# Second

# Hex

## Solstice Properties

## Mysteries: Book 1

### by A.M. Burns

See what A.M. Burns is up to.
Visit his website www.amburns.com
Sign up for his email list

Copyright 2020 © MysticHawker Press
http://www.mystichawker.com/

ISBN: 978-1-945632-70-9

Edited by Robert Brownson

Cover art by Fae Kelly

Other Books by A.M. Burns

Solstice Properties Mysteries
1: Second Story Hex
2: Watchtower WooWoo
3: Mid-Century Monster

Shifter Force
1: Visions of Rage
2: Visions of Shadows
3: Visions of Stars

Yellow Sky Coven:
1: Blood Moon Yellow Sky
2: Dark Stars of Dallas

Stand Alone Books:
The Black Fin Case

YA Books:
Coyote's Pup

Familiar Series:
1: Familiar Path
2: Familiar Spirit

Tempest Academy:
Prologue:
Running in a Pack
Into the Sky

# 1

Sweat coated Cinnamon "Cin" Kilkari as she forced her way through the final stretch in her morning yoga class. She'd joined the class a few months earlier when her husband Chad had gotten on a weight loss and fitness kick. They'd both lost a decent amount of weight, but Chad was literally shedding the pounds and it often felt like Cin was having to forcefully evict each ounce of fat that wanted to keep residence on her thighs.

"Okay folks, that's it for today." Shelby Foster, their friend and yoga instructor, bent over backwards and did a handstand to wave at the class as they picked up their towels and wiped sweat from their glistening bodies.

There were times Cin had to struggle to not hate Shelby for being so much more flexible than the rest of the world. But she was thirty-five and childless. A couple of kids would take the flexibility right out of her, but that was unlikely to happen.

"Come on, Cin. We need to get rolling." Chad wiped his towel over his neck and arms. His neck was almost as small as it had been when they met in college, but his arms were bigger than ever. For a man in his forties, he was looking almost as good as he had in his twenties. The edge of maturity sat on him perfectly. He wasn't one of those guys who was going to age badly, at least if he kept up the fitness. His full-moon activities didn't hurt either. Although they didn't know much about them before Chad had been attacked, Cin couldn't recall ever hearing about a fat werewolf.

"Don't we have time to run by the house for a quick shower?" Cin ran her towel through her long red hair and frowned. She couldn't stand the idea of spending the rest of the busy day they had ahead of them with sweat-slicked hair. Chad wouldn't mind. His short black hair didn't show the sweat the way hers did. He could literally change clothes, walk through a bit of cologne, and be fine. Nobody would even suspect he'd spent an hour stretching and sweating.

Chad glanced at his phone. "If we hurry."

Cin flashed Shelby a quick thumbs up. "Great class Shelby, see you tomorrow."

"Thanks, you two." Shelby returned the gesture. "Keep up the good work, you're awesome."

If there was one thing Cin didn't feel, it was awesome. She was hot, tired, and sweaty. Even though they had a new handyman to interview and a house to look at, she was already done with people for the day and was tempted to let Chad handle everything, but then they wouldn't get the best deal possible. Chad was a great front man for their business, but he was still learning how to get the most out of every situation. He was charming; with his sexy smile and twinkle in his eye, he could tell a tenant they were being evicted, and they'd thank him and bake him cookies he shouldn't eat. If she did the same thing, with the same twinkle and smile, she was called a bitch and a few other things. But he'd also agree to things too fast and not spot some of the problems in houses that she could. She was going to need to clean up and face the day. If she was lucky, she'd be done by two or three and able to go crawl into a book until it was time for her to throw the steaks on the grill for dinner.

# Second-Story Hex

Cin slipped the key into the office door. The shower had helped, as had a bit of fun with Chad. As they continued their midlife realignment, as Chad liked to call it, they'd rediscovered things they'd lost during their thirties when he'd been a cop and she'd worked the local bookstore part-time and been a full-time mother. She couldn't complain about most of it, although there were a couple of nights a month, during the full moon, when things were more different than they had ever been.

"Five minutes early." Chad ran an eager hand up her back, leaving warm tingles in its wake. "We didn't have to hurry in the shower."

Cin turned and gave him a quick kiss. "I'd rather be five minutes early, than two late. We're interviewing this new guy, and we've got to set a standard first thing. Don't want him to think we're not going to take things seriously by being late to his interview." She turned on the lights and walked into the outer office.

There was a desk for a receptionist that they might hire if they ever got big enough to warrant one. Since Solstice Properties was a small property-management firm that sidelined on flipping houses in Cottonwood Colorado, they weren't large enough to need more than the two of them and a couple of handymen who they often just contracted out for. But having taken on a ski chalet just east of Wolf Creek, they were needing a bit of full-time help, thus the interview they were racing to meet.

"He probably would've sat out in his truck for a few more minutes." Chad flipped the light switched on.

Cin spun back toward the door and looked out into the shared parking lot. "Chad, do you think that was him?"

"Blue truck, a bit banged up, but still running good. No

smell of excess oil. Decent tires. Driver a little neater than the truck. Blond hair, short beard, matches his Facebook profile. Yeah, I think that was him, and he's gotten out of the truck and is heading this way." Chad relayed all of the information on the man and his truck without turning around. As a cop he'd always been observant. Since the attack by a rogue werewolf a year earlier, his senses had grown to an irritating level of acuteness, even when he wasn't furry.

Cin dashed into her office. "I knew we should've been faster."

"You were the one who wanted to take a shower." Chad followed her into her office.

"And I'm glad we did." Cin hated being rushed to meet new people. Folks who knew her knew she'd either be on time, or close to it. She was always worried that new people might think she was running late when she rushed in two minutes early.

She started booting up her computer knowing she'd have had more time to glance over her emails if they'd been faster.

Chad grabbed his spare chair from the corner she always pushed it into to get it out of her way. They both had chairs in each other's office, since they liked to be on the same side of the desk when talking to people.

"I'll go let him in." Chad headed out of her office before the outer office door opened. His hearing drove her nuts sometimes.

Once Chad was out of the office, Cin took a second and pulled out the palm-sized mirror she kept in her top desk drawer to always make sure she looked decent before someone came into her office. Her makeup was fine, but a lock of hair had come out from behind her ear. She flicked it back into place and returned the mirror to the drawer as the sounds of Chad greeting their interviewee came from the front office.

Seconds later, Chad led the man, who was about the same size as he was, but a few inches broader, into her office. He had mid-length blond hair and a neatly-trimmed matching beard. There were a few laugh lines around his blue eyes as he smiled.

"Cin, this is Regulous Samson," Chad introduced them as he made his way around the desk to his chair.

Standing, Cin reached across the desk to shake his hand.

He had a strong calloused grip. "Most people call me RJ, it's less of a mouthful."

With her kids and herself preferring nicknames, Cin understood. She waved him to take the seat on the other side of the desk before settling into her own. "RJ, then. Are you new to Cottonwood? Can't say as I recall seeing you around town." Cottonwood wasn't the smallest town in the San Luis Valley, but it was far from the size of Denver or Colorado Springs. With Chad having been a police officer before the attack, and her working in the bookstore, they at least recognized, if not knew, a large percentage of the population.

RJ nodded. "We just moved to town a couple of months ago. Got tired of the growing traffic and population around the Springs and wanted a more rural environment."

Chad pointed at RJ thoughtfully. "Wait a minute. Did you buy the old Cowan place?"

"That's what people keep telling us." RJ chuckled. "We have never dealt with anyone named Cowan out there."

Cin tapped the desk. "The Cowans have been gone for years. Their family's tried time and again to sell it, but the deals always fall through at the last minute. Local legends say it's haunted."

RJ scratched his chin. "That might explain a few things. I'll mention it to AJ and we might have to look around for someone to purify the place if we can't deal with it ourselves."

"AJ, your other half?" From her digging through RJ's social media before the interview, she knew he was married to a man named AJ, but she didn't like people to know she cyberstalked them before meeting. Overall, she hadn't found anything disturbing in RJ's accounts.

"Yeah. He's a writer." RJ cocked his head slightly. "But aren't we supposed to be talking about my work here?"

There was a little sense of frustration in his tone, like he often took second seat to his husband, which made Cin want to know who AJ Samson was, or what pen name he used. That might take a bit more digging.

Chad flashed one of his disarming smiles. "Sure. So, from your resume, you've mostly done your own thing back in Colorado Springs. Ran your own handyman business for what… ten years."

RJ nodded. "That's right. Although my listings are still up on all the popular websites, and I'm still getting calls to do work back there, I'm a little tired of dealing with the extra work and taxes that come with self-employment. AJ pays enough in taxes for both of us. I just want to listen to other people for a while."

Chad laughed. "I think Cin's pretty good at bossing people around, if that's what you're looking for."

Cin flashed him a withering look. People did claim she was good at resting bitch face, and since she was a mother, she wasn't going to deny it, not for a second. "I'm good at providing direction when people need it. But it sounds like you're a pretty good self-starter. That's one of the things we're looking for. We just took on a condo outside of Wolf Creek. Not a ton of work most of the year, or that's how it's been in the past, but with their new push for year-round tourism, that's probably going to change. The guy who's been handling our rentals here in Cottonwood moved up there to be on-site. We're also looking at doing a bit of flipping, and need guys who can handle reno."

With a wide grin, RJ nodded. "I think I can handle that. We got lucky, and the new place didn't need much, but I've done some renos, particularly when the handyman jobs were slow."

"Good." Cin's phone beeped with her alarm. She swiped it off. "We're supposed to go over to a property this morning and take a look at it. We're not sure yet if it's going to be a flip or a rental. If you don't have plans, why don't you come out with us and take a look. Let's see how good your eyes are."

"I'll text AJ and let him know I won't be home for lunch."

"Then let's go." Chad stood first. "You can follow us over. It's just west of town."

Cin stood and gestured for the men to lead the way out of the office. She turned off lights as she went. On first impressions, she liked RJ. With any luck, he'd help them get a good feel for the house they were heading out to and they'd go ahead and hire him. Her first impressions were normally good. She hated having to interview people, not that they had a lot of people applying for the job after they listed it. Cottonwood was small enough that although not many people knew why Chad had left the police force, they all knew of his history, and even though they all liked him, working for an ex-cop made some people nervous. If they had known he was a werewolf, they would have been downright scared.

# 2

The house just west of town was... well, it wasn't run down... totally. It was going to need some work. Cin wasn't sure about the place as they pulled up in front of it. They hadn't done a lot of house flipping. Cottonwood just wasn't a great market like some of the towns that were closer to either Denver or ski resorts where the demand for modern housing was higher. In the rural area surrounding Cottonwood, people were used to houses that needed 'a little love' to be livable, but with several new agricultural companies moving into town, and a blooming marijuana business, more younger people were moving into the area, and they liked move-in-ready houses.

"Is this the same house we looked at the listing for?" Cin pulled up the listing they'd seen online and frowned. "Okay. It's the same place, but I don't think these pictures can be right. Well there's the same weathervane."

"What do you mean?" After he put the Subaru in park, Chad reached for her phone. "So the pictures were taken last winter. That big dust storm last month must've hit it hard. How did that weathervane survive? Must be up there well." He handed the phone back.

Cin glanced at her phone and back to the house that looked more than faded. There was something almost shabby about it, like it was waiting to be burned down and have something new rise from its foundation. The big crow on the weathervane seemed to be passing judgement from its high perch, then a gust of wind hit it and the metal bird spun away from them.

By the time they got out of the car, RJ was already to the corner of the house, his face a mask of concentration. "You're not wanting to try and do one of those two-week turnarounds like they do on TV, are you?"

Chad shook his head. "Nope. We understand the realities of life, plus sometimes it takes a couple of weeks to get specialty items delivered way out here."

"I can see that. Not like in Colorado Springs where if the regular places don't have it in stock, we can run to Denver." RJ tapped on the corner of the house and dust fell around him. "Yeah, a couple of weeks or more just on the outside."

Cin figured a couple of months, but then she wouldn't be the one on the ladders slapping paint across the wood. She ran the office, not the fieldwork. Maybe they'd be lucky and RJ and the crew they hired would be able to work miracles.

A smiling woman, their favorite real-estate broker, Marzie Campbell, strolled out of the house pausing to carefully navigate the couple of strides it took her to cross the small porch and come down the steps that looked like they were ready to collapse. She had her black hair pulled back a little more severely than normal, and the sunlight flashed off her large brown eyes.

"I see you found the place." She waited for them at the bottom of the stairs.

"Easy enough to get here." Chad flashed her a big smile.

Marzie smiled back like most people, particularly women, did when Chad turned on his charm.

"What's the story here?" Cin pulled up her note app so she didn't forget anything.

"It's been empty for a couple of years. Owners just disappeared and the county is selling it for back taxes." Marzie had her own phone out checking something.

Cin noted that with a nod. "I like that. Why hasn't someone snatched it up already?" She'd double check the cost, but county property taxes in didn't tend to be overly high.

"I can't answer that." Marzie started up the steps to the porch. "I just spotted the listing a few days ago and thought of you guys. You're always looking for a good investment, and this one has a lot of potential."

Chad and RJ followed behind them, occasionally knocking on a board or frowning as something creaked a little louder than it should.

A shiver ran through Cin as she crossed the threshold. She paused and glanced around. "Are you sure nobody lives here?" A house without tenants shouldn't have much of a threshold, and what she had just crossed was a definite sign of habitation. She came from a long line of witches, and could sense when something like a threshold was still intact.

Marzie nodded. "Positive. Like I said, owners seem to have vanished years ago, and they haven't been able to be found."

"Since it's just up for back taxes, I take it there isn't a lien holder." Chad slipped past Cin as she glanced around the dusty interior with the sunlight casting beams through the dust they kicked up. If there was one thing the residents of the San Luis Valley were used to, it was dust.

"Right." Marzie checked something on her phone. "The previous owners paid cash for it back in nineteen-ninety. Lived here over twenty years and vanished."

"This is going to take as much work inside as outside," RJ said softly, sounding more like it was to himself than all of them.

## Second-Story Hex

"Going to need a clean-out crew," Marzie said. "Looks like they left everything here when they left."

Chad took several deep breaths. "Just dust everywhere."

With Chad's subtle hint that they were alone, at least as far as his werewolf nose could tell, Cin tried to push the feeling there was someone, or something still living there as she walked deeper into the house. The living room was fairly small, but had a great view to the east. With a bit of squinting, or some binoculars, she might be able to see the Great Sand Dunes. From the way the couch and chairs were positioned, the previous inhabitants had enjoyed the view, which was probably spectacular in the morning with the sun rising over the mountains, and in the evening when things would be painted red and orange with the sunset.

"I've been through the house, and it may be a lot different after it's cleaned up, but I think there's going to be work in each room." Marzie moved to the side to let Cin and Chad inspect the place.

"I think that's an understatement, Marz," Cin said. They'd taken on some fixers, but this house was going to be a challenge, even at a cheap price. The repairs might make it hard to turn a profit flipping, but they might get the money back over time if they could get renters into it.

Over the next hour, they went through the house, checking every nook and cranny, getting RJ's input from time to time.

In the back yard, Cin stared up at the house. "Wait a minute. That wasn't in the listing."

Marzie looked up with her. "I thought I put that in there. It's not much, just a little efficiency apartment someone added on. I checked the original plans on file with the county and it's not there. Could make for a second source of income if you rent it out separately from the main house."

Cin studied the iron stairs that went up the outside of the house. They looked solid enough to hold her if she went up.

"Do you want me to try first?" RJ asked.

"That's nice, but let's send Chad up. If something happens, I've got an insurance policy on him." And she did. Even after he'd left the force, she'd kept the high-dollar policy on him, since she wasn't sure if something was going to happen to him during his monthly furry times. Better to take care of herself and the girls.

"I love you too, Dear." Chad flashed her a comical grin, then started up the stairs. They shook a little as he went, but held well.

"Looks safe," Cin called up.

"No problems." Chad replied. "Send Marzie up first. That way she can unlock the door and we don't have all of us on the stairs. That might not be a good idea."

"Right." Cin waved Marzie to the steps. "After you."

Chad was on the small porch staring out into the yard, his nostrils flared.

Cin looked out over the tall green buffalo grass and then back at her husband. "What's wrong?"

"There's a dead body in the yard." Chad swung over the porch railing and jumped down into the yard.

Halfway up the steps, Marzie was staring at him open-mouthed.

"Yoga does wonders, Marz, you should try it." Cin hated when Chad did something wolfie and she had to cover.

RJ nodded slowly. "Yeah. Yoga."

"It's right here." Chad pointed down at the ground at his feet. "A few feet down, but I can definitely smell it."

"Okay." Cin knew better than to argue with Chad's nose. If he said they had a dead body in the back yard, there was a dead body. She pulled out her phone and dialed 911. Her hopes for an afternoon with her book just went out the window. She glanced up at the door to the efficiency. She wanted to get in there more than ever, but that would have to wait until after the police were done with the yard and house.

# Second-Story Hex

Maybe, if she were lucky, she could get some knocked off the back taxes for there being a dead body on the property.

# 3

The Alamosa County Sheriff came quickly. Even though Chad had been part of the Cottonwood police force for fifteen years, Cin was always surprised at how quickly the cops showed up when he called. If the pizza guy was half as fast, it would make calling for a steaming pepperoni pie all the more appealing.

Within an hour of her call, a backhoe and coroner were out back of the house working on locating the bodies that Chad was positive were there. He had to reassure Sheriff Jackson that it wasn't just deer bones that some cougar or coyote had buried there. Somehow they managed to do all of it without Marzie overhearing.

During that time, Cin had been torn between keeping the real estate agent occupied and talking with RJ who was taking things in relative stride. Since Sheriff Jackson had asked for all of them to remain there, even if the scene was years old, he wanted statements from everyone, if they found bones.

"Stop!" shouted the Coroner, a young guy who looked like he had been dissecting frogs in high school the previous week.

"Whatcha' got, Dolon?" Jackson turned from where he'd been talking with Chad and the two men hurried over.

Unable to resist, Cin followed with RJ in tow. She didn't doubt Chad's nose had spotted something nobody else had been able to, but she always liked being able to confirm. No matter what kind of other-worldly strangeness entered her life, she liked confirmation. Spells and such were just words and gestures until they showed some kind of physical results.

Dolon lay on the ground and reached into the hole the backhoe had been working on. "Looks like finger bones." His voice was slightly muffled from his angle and having his head in the hole.

"So we've got bodies." Jackson shook his head. "All right. This entire place is locked down until we find out how many." He looked over his shoulder at Marzie. "No more showing of this place for a while."

Marzie raised her hands in retreat. "Definitely. Won't be able to sell this place now. County's just going to have to bulldoze it and put in a park, or a parking lot. Park works better since no point in a parking lot out here."

"Won't be that bad." Cin patted her friend on her shoulder. "Let's see if we can work a deal with the county."

Chad looked up from the hole with the body and shot her a questioning look.

Cin nodded back.

"I don't know, but we can try." Marzie pulled out her phone and started working on something. After a moment she looked up. "They're not normally really quick about getting back to me. I'll let you know when I know something."

"Sounds great." Cin turned her attention to Jackson. "I know you boys are good at jawing for days, but some of the rest of us have work to get done. When can we leave?"

"Still need to get statements from the four of you, since you found the body and all." Jackson put his hands in his pockets and looked like a kid working up the nerve to ask his mother something he didn't really want to. Even though the sheriff was the oldest person in the yard, other than the backhoe operator, whose long gray bread and frail body made him look like he should be kicked back on a porch with a glass of tea, or bottle of beer, and not digging up bodies in the middle of the afternoon, Jackson still pulled off the kid look.

If Cin hadn't known how controlling Jackson's wife was, she'd have thought the sheriff was worried about her getting mad. Lucille Jackson was active in a lot of Cottonwood's civic groups and most of the town's women were familiar with her way of plowing through everything to get what she wanted, and that included ruling her husband with an iron fist.

"If it isn't a problem, you could go by the station and give them," Jackson suggested. "It's not far from your office."

Cin gave him a warm smile. "Sure, Sheriff. I'll do that on my way back into town."

RJ pulled out his phone. "I'll need the address, but I can stop by as soon as we leave."

"Can I do it this evening?" Marzie asked. "I've got another showing in half an hour. It's on the eastern side of town, so I need to get moving."

"That's fine, Ms. Campbell," Sheriff Jackson said after he gave RJ the address.

"Hon, do you mind if I hang out here for a bit?" Chad asked. There was an excitement in his eyes that hadn't been there since he left the force.

Cin didn't have it in her to tell him no. "If the sheriff can give you a ride home, that'd be fine."

Jackson looked nervous again. He was one of the few people outside of immediate family who knew about Chad's attack. Most regular humans didn't know for sure about the existence of magical things like werewolves, vampires, and witches. A fair number of law enforcement did, but they tended to keep it quiet for fear that everyone else would freak out and cause trouble. From the look on his face, Jackson wasn't sure he trusted Chad to not eat him on the drive back to town.

"Sure. I can do that." Jackson didn't sound too relaxed.

Chad grinned his most disarming grin, at least the one he used with men. The one he reserved for women didn't often have the same effect with straight guys. "Thanks, Sheriff." He let out a satisfied sigh. "You know, I've missed this, a lot."

Cin patted him on the shoulder. "I know, sweetie. If you're going to be late for dinner let me know."

She turned around to tell Marzie goodbye, but the real estate broker had already reached her car and was getting in. Of all of them, Marzie had been the most freaked out about finding the skeletons, and that made Cin wonder if it had to do with more than just the delay in making a sale.

"If you want to follow me—" Cin looked at RJ "—I can lead you to the sheriff's office. It's a couple blocks from the office. Once we get done, we can go ahead and get your new-hire paperwork done."

RJ brightened. "I got the job?"

Chad mouthed. "We're hiring him?" Then flashed her a thumbs up.

"Yes. You were making some good suggestions before we stumbled onto the bodies, and then you didn't freak out over something strange. I think we can work well together." She hoped his constitution with the strange held. They were always stumbling onto something odd, but the bodies were a first.

**4**

Cin hadn't even closed the door to their modest split-level home when her eldest daughter, Charlotte, who decided she was going to be called Char years earlier, bounded down the stairs with the energy only a seventeen-year-old could have.

"Mom, Grandma says you found a skeleton today, and it's going to cause trouble," Char burst out as Cin was setting her purse on the small table near the door.

"Oh, Grandma's been telling on me again." Cin was never sure what was more irritating, that the ghost of her mother continued to be a constant influence in their lives, or that she spent a lot more time talking with Char than she did with Cin.

"Oh, Mom, you know she gets bored and just likes to follow us around so she can continue to have anchors in the real world." Char rolled her eyes dramatically. "Being dead sounds like it's incredibly sad."

Cin continued down the entry hall and toward the kitchen. "It wouldn't be so sad if she'd let us do the ritual that would open the way to her next life." Ever since her mother's ghost had shown up a couple weeks after her death from natural causes, she'd resisted any efforts from Cin to get her to move on. It wasn't that Cin didn't like having her mother around, but she worried that something more was going on than a simple case of a spirit wanting to stay with her family. Most families weren't as sensitive to the unknown as Cin and the girls.

"If you keep finding dead bodies when you go out to buy a house, you're going to need me around." Her mother materialized in the middle of the kitchen with her arms crossed and a frown. "Honestly, Cin, I don't understand why you are so set on getting rid of me. Most women would love having their mothers around to provide support and advice long after their physical bodies are gone. And since I don't have to worry about eating that strange diet you have the family on, it's a major win for me."

Cin shook her head. "Mom, a lot of people have gone keto, and it's not weird. Besides, Chad finds it easier to eat low carb, even when he's not close to a full moon." She made a point to walk through her mother's spectral form, because she knew it upset her.

Her mother huffed. "I thought I raised you to have respect for the lives you take when you eat, and to make sure to eat lots of vegetables and breads. They're on the earth to provide sustenance just like meat."

Opening the freezer and pulling out pork chops for dinner, Cin shook her head again. She was tired and not in the mood to rehash old arguments. Her mother had always had something to complain about, and being a ghost hadn't changed that in the least. "Mom, why were you following us today?"

"The girls weren't up to anything interesting in school, and didn't need my help on tests, so I had to have something to do. Was I just supposed to sit around and watch the roses grow? I love them, but it's not like they grow much as I sit and watch them. Besides, if I had done that when I was alive, people would've said I was being a little neurotic."

As she started hot water filling the sink to thaw the

chops, Cin resisted sighing, as anything like sighing was sure to set her mom off worse than she already was. She was going to have to talk to the girls again about letting their grandmother help them on tests at school. It wasn't classic cheating, but for young witches, it was pretty close.

"But I thought you might like to know that handsome young man you interviewed this morning has the glow about him." Her mom settled herself on the kitchen counter. It was a place nobody was prone to walking through her. "I wonder if we know his family."

Cin dropped the zip locked chops in the water and turned to stare at her mother. "RJ? I didn't pick up anything unusual about him."

"If you ate more vegetables, you'd be more sensitive, Dear. All that meat leaves you too grounded."

Rubbing her forehead, Cin was determined to be nice. "Mom, is he going to be a problem? We just hired him, but I can find a reason to let him go."

Her mother waved the comment away. "Don't worry about that, I'm sure he's a nice young man. Nothing bothersome in his aura, all bright and clear."

There were handy things about having her mother haunting them. As a ghost, she was a lot more sensitive to things like auras and people with magical gifts. Cin had to be in just the right frame of mind to see auras, and hadn't been that relaxed in years.

"But tell her about the bodies," Char prompted. "That's the cool stuff. She's hired handymen before, but never found a body, let alone two."

"Chad said there were two." Cin leaned against the counter by the sink. "What more do you know?"

"Not much." Her mother sighed. If there was one thing she didn't like admitting, it was that she didn't know something. "I couldn't get into the house. The threshold's still intact."

Cin nodded. "I thought so when I went in. It felt like

someone was still living there. But the place is dusty as all get out."

"Sweetie, this is Cottonwood, Colorado. I doubt the Sahara Desert has more dust than we do."

Char laughed. "Grandma, you do remember that the Sahara is more dirt than dust."

"And you should remember that it's not nice to correct your grandmother." Cin's mother pointed a ghostly finger at her granddaughter. "But I'd say there's either a person, or a ghost living in that house. If not living, then at least spending a lot of time there."

Cin frowned. "Mom, most ghosts aren't strong enough to leave a threshold intact. I mean, I think you could've, if you'd decided to haunt your own house instead of us, but you're an exemption to the basic rule."

"Our family is exceptions to a lot of rules, Dear. You know that." Her mother crossed her arms. "Anyway. The spirit, or spirits aren't with the bodies, I would've been able to tell that, but there's someone or something living in that house you're trying to buy."

Thinking back over what they'd seen in the main house, nobody had been in there in years. Other than Marzie's, there weren't any footprints on the hard floors. They hadn't made it into the second story efficiency. Chad had been really adamant about preserving the integrity of the crime scene. They'd mostly stayed near their cars until the sheriff arrived, then stayed out of the way as they excavated. Were there answers in the efficiency? But even if there was someone living there, it wouldn't explain the threshold at the front door. The efficiency was set up as a separate living quarters and should have its own threshold. She wanted to get back out there and check things over, but knew Chad was going to make her wait until the officials were done with the site.

The front door opened and closed.

Before Cin could head toward the hall, Chad's voice rang out. "Honey, we're home."

There was a skittering of shoes on hardwood, then their youngest, fourteen-year-old EEEK. Like her sister, she opted for a nickname and had gone with her initials, shortening Esmeralda Elizabeth Elena Kilkari down to something she felt was suitably original. Her short red hair was a contrast to Char's longer, blonder locks, but beyond that there was no doubting they were sisters, and Cin's offspring.

"Mom, was Dad pulling my leg about the skeletons in the yard of the new house?" EEEK stopped halfway between the two and looked back and forth. "Oh, hi Grandma."

"It's nice that someone in this family remembers how to respect their elders." Char's mother turned and smiled at EEEK.

"Oh, is Charity here?" Chad entered the kitchen. Even after his attack, he hadn't gained enough sensitivity to be able to feel the ghost.

Cin gestured to where her mother still sat on the counter. "Yes. She was just explaining that there is a threshold at that house and she couldn't enter."

Chad grinned. "Maybe we need to move in tonight."

"If he's going to get rude, I'm leaving." The ghost crossed her arms again and glared at her son-in-law.

"Be nice, Chad. She might have some useful information." Cin often found herself standing between her husband and her mother. In life, they'd gotten along fairly well, but something had changed in Chad when Charity Fisher had failed to stay dead. And after his attack, her patience with him had dropped to a low level, making things harder for Cin. Even three years after her death, Cin still hadn't made any headway on getting them to get along.

"Okay." Chad looked toward where Char had gestured. "I'm sorry Charity. We're always open to your opinion."

"Except for your diet. Too much meat." Her expression softened.

# Second-Story Hex

Cin didn't respond.

"Okay, about the skeletons." Her mom sighed like she was disappointed that Cin hadn't taken the bait to continue the argument. "I don't know much more. I can't say that I've ever seen bones that devoid of life before."

"Devoid of life?" Cin pondered the phrasing. "So they were more than just dead? How is that possible?"

"That might call for a bit of research. You and the girls can go digging into the books and see what you can find." Her mother smiled and faded from view.

Cin let out a relieved sigh. "That wasn't overly helpful, but it might give us a starting point."

Chad glanced around. "I take it she's gone?"

"Yeah, Dad." EEEK put her hands on her hips and stared at him. "I don't get why you and grandma can't get along a little better. She's just being nice by stopping by like she used to. Sure she can't bring us stuff anymore, but she's nice to talk to."

"Really, Dad, just because you can't see her like the rest of us, doesn't mean you can be mean." Char backed up her sister. "You and Mom have told us for years to be nice to everyone, and that should include dead people. They can't help it they're dead."

Chad looked at Cin quietly begging for back up.

She shook her head. "They're your kids too." Then she couldn't take his sad puppy look any longer. "Okay, girls, you've both probably got homework. Go get it done before dinner, then we'll go down into the library and see what we can find."

Both girls grinned and ran up to their rooms.

Chad closed the distance between them and gave Cin a quick kiss. "Sometimes I think you know how to manipulate all of us way too easily."

Cin put a hand to her chest and gave him her best innocent look. "Who me?"

"Yes you."

"So, do we know who the bodies are?"

Chad stepped away from her and went to the fridge to get a bottle of beer. He allowed himself one, as long as they weren't too close to the full moon. They'd found out through talking with the alphas in Denver that alcohol and full moons didn't mix real well, particularly for younger werewolves.

"We don't know for sure. Jackson's going off the logical and figuring they're the couple who disappeared from there a few years back. They're going to run some DNA testing, but that's going to take a while. We're supposed to treat the place as a crime scene while we're doing demo."

"Wait a minute…We?" She pointed between the two of them.

"And RJ and anyone else we bring into the site." He grinned. "And you might even be impressed. I offered to do it for the back taxes."

"And Jackson agreed?" Cin hugged him.

"He did, but he's got to get the county to process it." He put his hands on her hips and kept him close. "Since it's different departments, might take a day or two for the final approval, but it's going to be cheaper than calling in the Canyon City CSI team. Since I got sent to the FBI crime scene course right before the attack, I've got the official credentials to not screw things up. Although Jackson isn't keen on my changes, he's worked with me before, and trusts me as an officer."

"Good job. Sometimes, you're phenomenal." She kissed him again. "Thanks for saving us a bunch of cash. Now we might be able to turn a profit even having to totally redo that place." She loved it when he pulled a rabbit out of his hat and surprised her.

# 5

Cin opened the door to the library, and the girls followed her in. It was their little magical version of a she shed, or a man cave, since it was actually in the house and not in the backyard. Chad had his own private area next to theirs, but he normally just used it on the nights of the full moon when he wasn't sure if he'd be able to hold it together. Right after his attack, they'd moved his TV and stereo system out and up to the living room so he didn't break them. Also during those nights, Cin and the girls didn't spend time in their library. The howling wasn't conducive to quiet study time.

"So what are we looking for exactly?" Char went to the closest bookcase.

"Not exactly sure. Remember how Grandma phrased it, devoid of life." Cin sat at the desk that was between the bookshelves. "We need to find a reference to that, or something like that."

"You know, it might make this all easier if we had a database of everything we could just type in something and get answers out quickly and easily." EEEK went to the bookshelf on the other side of Cin.

"That might be something you two can do during summer break that starts next month, between camps that is." Cin didn't want to admit that it was a great idea that she'd thought about many times herself. Unfortunately, her life was so busy that even trying to catalogue everything her mother had left them into a basic binder was more daunting than she wanted to deal with.

Char huffed. "Thanks, Esmeralda Elizabeth Elena, you know how they are. We bring up a good idea, and it's suddenly work for us."

EEEK stuck her tongue out at her sister.

Cin frowned and stared over her shoulder at her eldest. "We keep up having attitude issues, and I can throw in restocking the wild harvested herbs, dusting everything in the house, and weeding the garden."

"I guess we're going to be spending nights looking for what we need." Char thumped a book down in front of Cin without further comment on her degenerating summer free time.

"If this doesn't work, yes." Cin pulled out a small cauldron from the shelf in front of her. There was a small chance she could get the information they needed, but if they could, it could keep them from stumbling into something she'd rather not deal with.

"Cool!" EEEK leaned Cin's shoulder. "Spells!"

"Do we need a circle?" Char leaned against the bookshelf.

"Not for this. It's a simple spell, not a summoning." Cin reached for a couple of herbs on the shelf above her desk. She sprinkled them into the cauldron before getting the fireplace lighter from the shelf she'd taken the cauldron from. Since there was already a marble cutting board that made up the center of her desk, she didn't worry about scorching anything as she did her magic.

She pulled a small slip of paper from the shelves, and handed it to Char. "Okay, Dear, you get to start. What are we looking for?"

"Any reference to devoid of life." Char pulled a pen from the dragon-shaped pen holder on the desk.

# Second-Story Hex

"Yes." Cin nodded, happy that she'd trained her daughters' talents so well that they knew what she wanted and she no longer had to spell things out to them. They still had house rules about the girls doing magic without her being there, but they were both adept at that thing that set them apart from most of the people around them.

Char jotted on the paper before passing it to EEEK who repeated the process before passing it to Cin.

After she added her own, devoid of life, Cin added, locate above Char's writing.

"Okay, girls, let's see what happens." Cin drew power from the earth around them. One of the advantages to having the library in the basement was ease of accessing earth energies.

Char and EEEK added their own power to the paper, and it shimmered slightly before Cin clicked the lighter and held the paper into the flame. As it caught fire, she dropped it into the cauldron and the smoke started to tendril out. Three columns of gray smoke that smelled of lavender and eyebright coiled around them before heading to the bookshelves. There, the smoke moved up and down, back and forth before forming arrows that pointed to three books.

"Okay girls, grab them quick before the smoke fades." Cin smiled as the girls grabbed the books their magic had indicated.

Once they had the tomes, Cin covered the cauldron with its small lid. The smoke ended and the tendrils evaporated.

"Now, let's see what we've got here."

"Do you want us to help look?" EEEK asked.

"From over my shoulder." Cin opened the first book. "You, my dear, are easily distracted by things that sound like something you might want to try out."

EEEK crossed her arms and pouted. "I know we're not to do magic unless you're with us." She dropped her voice and glared at her sister. "I listen."

31

Char was glaring back.

Cin sighed and decided to not interfere with her daughters. She was well aware of Char's simple experiments in casting on her own. When she thought back to her own teenage years, Cin couldn't deny that she'd been a bit rebellious to her mother's rules on such things. The biggest concern was, she'd grown up in a more innocent age. The girls were so much more likely to get caught doing something woowoo. Although magic and tech often didn't mesh, things kept popping up online that couldn't be easily explained away. It made the paranormal community nervous. When people were nervous, they got fearful, and fear made people do stupid, reactionary things. She didn't want her kids wrapped up in something stupid because they didn't keep their differences to themselves.

"Okay. If you spot anything I miss, stop me. We're scanning quickly because you girls have school tomorrow." Cin made it past the entry pages the first book and into the listing of spells. Based on the title of the book, 'Popular Rites of Passage' it was going to be fairly dry, as most of the books in their library were. After she saw that the first three rites were fertility rituals, it was fairly obvious that the tome was going to be life magic.

EEEK wrinkled her nose. "I'm so glad I'm not going to have any kids. This sounds gross." She pointed at the fourth ritual that was fairly graphic for couples who were having particular difficulties in getting pregnant.

The next set of rituals were for birth.

"Really? Mom, we know all about this." EEEK continued to complain. "Did you and Grandma do any of these before we were born? They still sound awful."

"No, well, unless Grandma did something without telling me." At the time, she was limiting the witchy part of life, for Chad's sake. He'd known all about her magic, but hadn't been as comfortable with it as he was since his own change in status to beyond human.

## Second-Story Hex

"Good." Char leaned on Cin's chair. "I don't want to think about you and grandma doing some of this." She gestured to the spell Cin was flipping past that was designed to make the delivery easier.

They went on for a few more pages, skipping past rituals for first words, first steps, starting school, and more.

When they reached the passage rituals of first period, Char tapped the page. "Hey, we did this, or something close to this."

Cin patted her hand. "We did, for both you girls. This is a lot more important than things like first steps and such."

EEEK looked at the page. "Oh yeah, I remember this one. Mine was right after Dad's accident. I was really glad he wasn't there. That would've been beyond gross."

"He wouldn't have wanted to see it either." Cin sighed and kept turning pages. Most of the rituals became less and less important, things for new jobs, new homes, other things that were forms of passage in everyone's life, but nothing for devoid of life. The logical thing was that they were going to find the reference in the back of the book, with death rites, but she didn't want to risk missing something by skipping to the end.

"Hey, when do we get to do this one for you?" Char stopped Cin from turning the page from the menopause rite. "You should be ready to be a crone, right?"

Cin frowned and turned the page. "Not for a few more years, yet." She didn't bother mentioning that as long as her mother continued to haunt them, they had a crone in their little family circle. She was in no rush to hit that spot in her life.

"Wait." EEEK leaned over Cin's arm and touched the book. "There it is."

With a soft smile, Cin patted EEEK's arm. "Thanks, Sweetie. That's it indeed." She scanned over the ritual that had mentioned devoid of life, in the description. It was a simple death ritual that was performed when someone was devoid of life. It opened the way for a trapped soul to enter the other world and proceed on to their next life.

"That's not what we're looking for is it?" Char bent so her elbow was on the desk, in an awkward position that was only not uncomfortable to a teenager.

Cin pulled out a piece of paper and slipped it into the book to mark the spell. "Maybe, maybe not. It doesn't explain why the bones are devoid of life, but it might help us lay any spirits around the bones to rest. Remember, that all spirits need to go on to their next life, they'll be happier then." Cin was thankful her mother couldn't cross the protective wards of the library without an invite. She wasn't in the mood to have the debate about her passing, again.

"Except for Grandma," EEEK said. "She seems perfectly happy with us. Maybe when we're all gone, she'll be ready to go on too."

"I hope she leaves before then." Cin finished scanning through the rest of the rituals in the book without finding any other reference to the strangely specific phrase.

Over the next couple of hours, they pored through the other books, with only a slightly more useful reference in one. There was nothing about how to make someone, or something, devoid of life, which was how Cin was thinking about things. If her mother had chosen that particular phrase, it was important; she just needed to figure out how, and why. By the time they all needed to go to bed, she wasn't in the mood to try and get her mother to explain it. Occasionally dealing with ghosts could be like dealing with dementia patients—they could be easily scattered and distracted.

# 6

"You feel better after stretching. You feel better after stretching. You feel better after stretching." Cin muttered her yoga mantra as her body complained with each new pose and sweat began to run down between her breasts. She wasn't in the mood to be social or active, but she and Chad had their daily rituals, and life was better with patterns, as it gave her time to not think too much about what she was doing and get going. Often, by the time they finished yoga class, she was awake and ready to face the day. After an evening of poring over magical tomes with the girls, and then restless sleep, she wasn't ready to face anything beyond more than being cozy with her comforter.

"Okay, that's it for today," Shelby sounded too perky to live, but at least didn't do her little handstand wave trick as everyone plopped down on their mats to wipe their brows and mutter about what a slave driver she could be.

Cin wiped her towel across her face, and hoped to wake up after a quick shower. One of the advantages of living in a small town was it wasn't far from the only yoga studio to her house.

Beside her, Chad held his pose a little longer, before bending over and picking up his towel.

"You know you're a show-off sometimes," Cin muttered at him just loud enough for him alone to hear.

"Only for you." He reached down to give her a hand up from her mat, then gave her a quick kiss.

"Hey, did you two really find bodies when you went to look at that new house yesterday?" Shelby came over, mopping her own brow.

"Yeah. Looks like the couple who disappeared might never have left." Cin turned and stepped out of Chad's embrace. "Okay, we don't know if it was the couple... I don't even know their names. Marzie didn't say." She looked back at Chad. "Did Jackson?"

Chad looked thoughtful, then shook his head. "Can't say as he did. That's odd."

"It is, when you stop and think about it," Cin said.

"That was that place out on CR3, right, the Old Stone place?" Shelby seemed to know more than either of them.

"Maybe. What do you know?" Cin draped her towel over her shoulders.

"Well, depends on if it's the same place. But before I moved into town a couple of years ago to be closer to this place, I lived out that way, actually right next door to them. It's got that second-story efficiency in the back." Shelby wiped the sweat from her arms.

"That should be the place, unless there's lots of houses out that way that have second-story rooms built on." Chad walked over and plopped down in one of the brightly-colored beanbag chairs that lined the back of the room.

Cin and Shelby followed him. Although it was nice to get a little more info, Cin really wanted to go get a shower. Luckily, they didn't have anyone due at the office for another couple of hours.

"Well, the Stones were a fairly quiet couple, mid-forties if I remember correctly." Shelby folded up into the beanbag chair next to him. "They both worked from home, which wasn't as common in the nineties as it is today."

"Anything odd about them?" Cin asked as she settled into the bright pink blob of a seat and tried to shift just right, so her sore thighs weren't complaining as much.

Shelby sighed like the blue beanbag she sat in was the most comfortable chair she'd ever sat in. "Not really. They did seem to go through renters though. Never kept any for more than a few months. I mean that's not uncommon as people try and get the seasonal jobs available around here."

Cin nodded. She was well aware of the people who either came through to work the pot fields, or hoped to get jobs at one of the ski resorts, and hadn't realized they were really a bit far away, particularly in bad weather, to make Cottonwood, or any of the rural areas around it work for living and still hope to get to the slopes in a timely fashion.

"But back then it was a fairly quiet place, and even if people did come and go, it wasn't bad. I don't think the Stones put up with loud, obnoxious people, and even if they did, with Jackson living on the other side of the place, people minded their p's and q's."

Chad perked up. "Wait a minute, Sheriff Jackson used to live on the place next to the Stone house? He didn't mention that."

Shelby shrugged. "He and Lucille moved into town before I did. She was tired of listening to coyotes howling and owls screeching, and Jackson could never tell her 'no' about anything."

"I don't think anyone tells Lucille Jackson 'no' and doesn't live to regret it." Chad grinned slightly.

"Right." Shelby laughed. "But they moved to the city about the time the Stones disappeared. You don't think Lucille could've done something to them?"

It was Chad's turn to laugh. "Can you honestly see Lucille Jackson lowering herself to do something like burying the neighbors in their own yard?"

"No, but I can see her forcing the sheriff to do it after she killed them." Cin shivered.

"If it was Lucille, good luck finding any evidence

against her, she's good at covering her tracks," Shelby said.

Suddenly the sheriff offering to get the county to give them the house for doing his CSI work for him made a lot more sense. Even though Chad had the training, he was no longer a city official. Jackson would most likely take the report from him and mark it like it came from one of the deputies, if they found anything. If they didn't find anything, it was a lot cheaper for the county than coughing up the money to go over the scene. If they discovered something that Jackson didn't want to have exposed, it might also be a way for the evidence to disappear. Suddenly Cin didn't like the idea of taking the house.

Chad leaned toward Shelby. "You've got something on Lucille?"

Cin nodded. "Spill."

Shelby held her hands up to ward them off. "Nobody's hearing anything from me about her. She's apt to turn her evil eye my direction and that's something I don't want to deal with."

Evil eye? Cin thought back on her brief encounters with Lucille Jackson. She'd never picked up anything like that from her. She was a bit of a curmudgeon, but not a witch, although that would explain her tight control of her husband and the fear of women she inspired in him.

"You don't really think Lucille could have magic do you?" Cin asked.

Shelby shrugged. "I run a yoga studio. I understand that the universe isn't exactly how we perceive it. Do I think Lucille has magic? I don't know if I'd call it magic exactly, but we get out of the world what we're determine to take. If we want something strong enough, things sometimes fall into place to make it happen. We make our own magic."

Chad shot her a look to not push Shelby any further, as if to say We enjoyed our yoga with her and didn't need her to start looking at us in an attempt to see our differences. "Cin, we need to get rolling. Just remembered I need to stop by and see if that late renter has her payment ready."

Cin nodded. "Yeah, we should get." She worked her way up out of the beanbag chair, with much complaining from her thighs. "Shelby, keep your ears open. If you hear anything, let me know. We're still trying to decide on the house. Skeletons in the back yard can be a bit of a turn off."

Shelby stood up much more easily than Cin had. "Sure, but it's a nice little place out there. If the town starts expanding, might even go that way and make the land more valuable than the house."

"That's what I'd been thinking too." Chad all but jumped out of the squishy chair. Sometimes Cin was a bit jealous of her husband's improved physical skills after the attack, but she didn't want to endure the monthly full moon nights. "If we rent it out for a while, then when the property values swing up, we can sell it off making a great profit."

"Wait, who are you and what did you do with Chad?" Cin smiled at him. She was always teasing him about making bad choices.

"That last wealth-building seminar had an effect on me." He took her arm and steered her toward the door.

"See you guys in the morning," Shelby called after them.

Cin waved. "Always." She hoped her sleep would be better so she wouldn't hurt as much when she started twisting and bending to Shelby's instructions.

# 7

By the time they were ready to close up the office for the day, Cin's slight backache had turned into a roaring headache. All she wanted to do was go crawl into a tub, soak until the water was too cold to stand, and then get out and slither under the covers and sleep.

"We've got the end-of-the-year PTA meeting tonight," Chad announced.

Cin glared at him like he was some kind of monster who was determined to steal her last bit of happiness. "No."

"Yes. We need to get the girls, get something to eat, and go." He sounded like he hadn't spent the afternoon listening to her complain about every little thing that irritated her on the internet, her email, and just general life.

"Can we go get some dinner, and then you and the girls can go to PTA while I go home and fall over?" She turned off her computer, thankful the screen was no longer shining brightly on her face.

"Dinner, PTA, and then I'll give you a rubdown." He leaned against the door trying to look understanding and failing miserably.

"Dinner, bubble bath, rubdown, sleep." She stood and started toward him with the sinking feeling that she wasn't going to make much headway and was going to have to endure more people than she wanted to. Sometimes her core introvert made dealing with people harder than she liked to admit.

"Dinner, PTA, candle lit bubble bath, rubdown, and happy husband?" He raised his eyebrows suggestively.

"The way my brain is pounding, a happy husband better be content with a bit of cuddling before sleep." She stomped past him toward the outer office door.

"Lavender bubble bath it is." He reached the door and opened it before she had to.

She kissed the side of his face, just above his short beard. "Okay." She let out a long sigh, she hated PTA meetings, but at least they'd stopped trying to get her onto the board of anything.

"Cin, Chad!" A man shouted as they followed their seater from the buffet cashier toward their table.

Harvey Longtooth, Chad's old partner on the police force, was waving at them from the buffet line. He had an empty plate in his hand. "Fancy running into you two here."

"The steak house had a two hour wait," Chad replied. "Girls, go on to the table and get your drinks ordered." He caught the seater's gaze. "We'll both have sweet tea."

Harvey rolled his eyes. "Yeah, same here. I don't get it. Why does that always happen on PTA nights?"

"People trying to get out of going to the meeting by clogging the best food in town." Cin didn't mind expressing her opinion that the buffet was her second choice. Her head still hurt, and the cacophony of kids and parents in the restaurant didn't do much to help it. If they ate fast food, that would've been a quieter option. "At least if everyone sees them there, they can claim they didn't make the meeting due to circumstances beyond their control."

"CBTC." Harvey laughed. "How many people have

claimed that as a defense over the years? More than we can count."

Chad laughed with him. "Got that right."

"So I heard something about you guys buying the old Stone place out on CR three." Harvey took a couple of steps back from the serving counter so they weren't blocking access.

"Not yet, and not exactly buy," Chad said.

Harvey nodded. "Heard that too. Been some odd stuff going on out that way."

That caught Cin's attention and she hoped the conversation wasn't about to turn into a male jawing session. Although she knew men were afraid of women who spent too much time gossiping, the guys she knew, particularly cops and ex-cops, tended to be worse gossips than most women ever thought about being.

"What kind of stuff?" Chad dropped his voice since they were in public.

"Stuff. Hard to explain. Officially nobody's supposed to be living out there, but neighbors are reporting lights and stuff." Harvey hummed thoughtfully. "Only way I know is I was talking to Travis, you remember Jackson's newest deputy."

"And by newest, you mean the guy who's only had his job for about five years," Chad replied. "Yeah, I remember."

Char came up looking a little put out. "Can EEEK and I go ahead and get our dinner? The drinks are on the table."

Cin glanced over to where EEEK leaned against the table with her arms crossed looking like she was ready to say something. "Okay, yeah, you two eat."

"Thanks, Mom." Char waved for EEEK to join her as she stepped up to the serving counter and started loading her plate.

"He thought you might want to know about the lights and stuff," Harvey was still talking like he hadn't noticed Cin's quick interaction with Char.

"That's useful, but the inside of the house didn't look like there'd been anyone in it in years, well other than our real estate broker," Chad said.

"Oh yeah, still using Marzie? Did you hear that she filed an assault charge on a guy in Salida?"

Cin's jaw dropped and she whipped her head around from watching the girls to stare at Harvey. "Wait…what?" She was friends with Marzie. She should've known about something like that.

Harvey nodded. "Yeah. I heard about the report a few days ago. She's trying to keep it out of the news, but figures it's going to get around. You know how things are in Cottonwood."

"Everyone knows everything." Cin sighed. She wasn't going to have time to call Marzie until morning, unless… yes, she could do it during her bubble bath. They might be able to have a coffee after yoga.

"Right. But the officer who took the report called me to get a reference on Marzie, make sure she wasn't some kind of nut job. You know how easy it is for a woman to get upset and then file charges against any man who looks at her wrong."

Cin resisted the urge to growl at Harvey. He was a nice guy, but tended to be a bit of a misogynist. Chad had often put it down as just the way Harvey was raised by ultra-conservative parents and didn't know better.

"You do realize that a lot of women are just getting tired of putting up with guys' crap, don't you, Harvey? Sometimes an assault is actually an assault and needs to be reported." She glared at him so hard that Harvey took a couple of steps back and the stack of plates on the buffet fell over.

Chad put a hand on her arm. "Cin, if you would like to go ahead and get dinner."

She turned her gaze on him. "Don't do that, Chad." She

took a deep breath to rein in the anger bubbling around inside her. It had been years since her magic had lashed out like that and caused things to fly or fall. At least the stack of plates hadn't hurt anyone, and could've fallen without her help.

Raising his hands up. "I'm sorry, hon. I didn't mean anything."

Harvey sighed. "Look, why don't I call you tomorrow, we can grab lunch and catch up."

"Sounds like a good idea," Chad agreed.

Cin sighed. She wanted to hear if Harvey had more to say, but his making it sound like Marzie was just hysterical or something pissed her off. One of the plusses of running their own business was she didn't have to deal with people she didn't like. More than once, she'd had a bad feeling about a potential renter and turned them down on that, then heard later they'd beaten a spouse, or robbed someone. Harvey wasn't a bad guy, he just had some mixed-up beliefs. She'd let Chad go have lunch and see what more he could get out of his ex-partner.

Chad leaned in close as he spun her around to face the buffet counter. "Sorry about Harvey. You know how he can be."

"Yeah. I know how he can be." Cin let out a low breath. "I'm okay."

"Just glad you're not throwing plates at me." Chad chuckled and helped let more of the stress out of Cin.

She always thought it was awesome having a husband who knew how to defuse her. "If I'm throwing plates at you, you'll know it." She kissed his nose before asking the server for a few slices of roast beef. The noise of the place still bothered her, but she was doing what she could to block it out. She was worried about Marzie, but wanted to be someplace where she could give her friend her full attention before calling.

# 8

Quite swaddled the Valley Latte as Cin walked in. She was more refreshed than she'd been the previous morning. She'd slept decently, yoga had gone well, and she'd gotten a shower afterwards. Overall, she felt like a new woman.

Marzie sat at a small café table toward the back of the place. It had cleared out from the early morning rush, and most of the mismatched tables and chairs were deserted. Even the mosaic tile floor was cleaned of any of the spills that had surely happened from groggy patrons impatient for their early morning caffeine fix.

Cin ordered her extra-tall, extra-strong frothing drink, and instantly promised herself an extra helping of yoga, either before bed or after class the next morning. She didn't normally indulge, but the way Marzie sat staring at her table, not even looking up when the doorbell clanked to announce another customer, Cin knew she was going to be there for a while, and probably needed fortification, and cake was way off her diet.

While she waited for the barista to get the drink ready, Cin headed over to Marzie, who finally looked up as she reached the table.

"Hey, Cin," Marzie's voice lacked all of its normal vigor. Something was way wrong.

"Marzie." Cin held out her arms to offer the other woman a hug. She was never one who was quick to hug, but Marzie looked like she needed it.

Slowly Marzie stood and embraced Cin.

Cin stepped back and studied her friend "Marzie, you look rough."

A long sigh escaped Marzie and she sank back into her seat. The way she latched onto her cup showed she was desperate for warmth of any kind.

"Talk to me." Cin settled across from her and took her hand. "You weren't acting like this the other day at the house."

Marzie huffed. "The house. Cin, have you ever felt like you were cursed?"

Cin shook her head. "No, I can't say as I have. But I understand you're having a rough time of it."

"That doesn't start to explain it." Marzie closed her eyes. "The way things are going, I'm not surprised that we found skeletons in that back yard. Seriously. That's just the icing on the cake right now. I worry about asking if things can get any worse. With my current run of luck, the universe will take it as a challenge and see just what else it can throw at me."

"So, it's more than just the skeletons and the assault charges?" Cin let go of Marzie's hand to accept her drink from the barista who'd brought it over to the table as opposed to calling her to the counter the way they normally did. There were plusses to coming during a slow time.

Marzie nodded. "Where to start. You heard about the charges, but then Chad used to be on the police force here, so I guess the folks in Salida let him know, or something."

"His ex-partner told us when we ran into them last night at the buffet." Cin sipped her drink. Nearly perfect, like normal.

"I can see that. Two small towns in the mountains and the police folks are bound to talk to one another. I guess I should be lucky that not everyone knows everything else."

"Like what? Come on, Marzie. Don't keep leading me on. What else is going on?" Cin wasn't as close to Marzie as she was to some of the other women in town, but they'd been getting closer over the past year as Cin and Chad grew Solstice Properties.

"Okay, so it didn't even start with that butt of a client grabbing me in Salida, and then the police didn't want to take a report because I didn't have video evidence, and he didn't leave a mark." She took a sip of her drink. "Cin, I know what it feels like to have a guy get handsy. It was more than just a simple bump on the stairs."

"And I hope you can nail him to the wall." Cin had never had to deal with a client or customer making unwanted contact with her, but she understood it was a growing problem and more people needed to be held accountable for their actions. It wasn't just guys grabbing women, some ladies liked to grab the boys too.

"My lawyer's working on it. She says we shouldn't have a problem since this is the first time I've reported anyone, and I've been in real estate for over fifteen years."

"Wow, that long?" Cin thought back trying to remember a time Marzie hadn't been selling properties in the valley.

Marzie nodded. "Got my license right out of college. Things were just starting to pop here in the valley, and it seemed like a great time to go into it. Haven't regretted it until recently. Lately it just seems there's something majorly wrong with each house, and not just the houses. Jerry left me."

Cin set her cup down a little too hard and some of her hot cream splashed out onto her hand. She brought it up to her mouth and sucked it off, trying to cool the hot spot on her skin. "Wait a minute, Jerry left you? What happened?" Jerry and Marzie had been together almost as long as she'd been in real estate. He'd been one of her first clients and they had a son who was in the same grade as EEEK.

Marzie's face got hard. "Same old classic tale, younger woman, tighter butt, bigger tits. The divorce won't be final for another couple of weeks, and I've been trying to keep it quiet." She stared at her coffee cup. "I really don't want everyone to feel sorry for me. We've been covering his absence with his new job in Denver. I get to keep everything we had here, he gets the 401K and his car. With my job going well right now… as well as it can with skeletons showing up in yards, I'm not going to apply for support. Heck I supported him for years, didn't I?"

Cin patted her hand again. "Sweetie, you did more for him than most women would."

"I know." She squeezed Cin's hand. "But since this has been going through the works, it's been tons of little things. Pipes bursting while I'm showing houses. A pack of coyotes killing a deer during an inspection. It's like if anything at all can go wrong, it has. I've even had a contractor fall through a skylight while working on a roof. Luckily, he wasn't killed—well, that might've been cheaper. Cost my insurance over a hundred K by the time he was ready to go back to work."

"I heard about that one." Cin squeezed Marzie's hand back. "That wasn't your fault. Chad got with the building inspector after that and he said some of the shingles had been blown loose during that big wind storm we had a couple of months ago."

Marzie let go of Cin and took a sip of her coffee. "That's why he was on the roof in the first place. He had to get it repaired before we could sell it, and since I was the one who hired the crew, my insurance was responsible for it, not the owner. Like I said, I feel like I'm cursed or something."

Cin didn't want to admit Marzie did sound cursed. Sure everyone ran into bouts of bad luck from time to time, but her run sounded a bit extreme. Maybe later, when the girls got home, they'd consult with her mother and see if there was something they could, or should do. Sometimes doing magic for people without either asking, or having someone request help, things could go horribly wrong. The way things sounded the only way things could get worse was if a house fell on Marzie, or something similarly catastrophic. Then an idea hit.

"You know, if you believe in curses and that sort of thing, you might try stopping by that shop down on the square, Open Mind Books and Curios. Shelby, our yoga instructor, said they were a fairly upscale new age shop. They might have something to help break curses." She hated the idea of passing off magic for friends like that, but she kept her own witchiness on the down low. The last thing she wanted was a mob led by the latest radical clergy trying to make a name for themselves by bringing back witch burning.

Marzie pursed her lips. Then nodded. "Might not be a bad idea. I've never been in there, but they might have a candle or something to help me out. Thanks for the idea."

From the sound of it, if there was a curse, it was going to take more than just a candle to fix it, but if it wasn't, burning a candle might help Marzie relax a bit and positive things might start flowing her way again. Sometimes personal belief was stronger than any spell or curse that was cast on a person.

"So what else is going on? You look more tired than just skeletons, coyotes and a soon-to-be ex." Cin tilted her head slightly, after she took another sip of her coffee.

"That's about it." Marzie sighed and spread her hands. "Although, I have to tell you, the skeletons really shook me up. That's why I left as soon as the sheriff said we could go. I know Chad used to be on the force, so he's probably used to dead bodies, but I've never dealt with that before."

"Me too. I left right after you did. But I think we are going to take the place. Chad's working out a way for us to

**49**

go over the place so Jackson doesn't have to bring in the crime scene guys from Salida in exchange for the house."

Marzie frowned. "And then I don't get a commission on it. Not that it would be that much, since it's a tax lien sale, but really. See. I'm cursed." She picked up her coffee and drained it, dribbling some of the dregs down her pink blouse. She slammed the cup down hard on the table. "See. Cursed. Now I have to go home and change before I can show that place to the south of town."

Cin reached across the table again and patted Marzie's hand again. "Tell you what, if we get the deal, we'll cover your commission on the place. I mean, you did show it to us. We'll probably also need you to handle the paperwork to get it in our name."

A faint smile curled Marzie's lips. "Thanks. Have you guys decided if it's a flip or a rental?"

"Not yet. Chad's leaning toward rental, at least until that part of the county is on the upswing and we can make a real profit out of it. Renting we get even more out of it, even if we do have to go in and do some touch ups before selling. That won't be a huge deal."

"Logical thinking. Sounds like Chad is really taking to the business-minded entrepreneur role well."

A soft chuckle escaped Cin. "He's trying. It's taking a lot of prodding to get him moving the right way. He's always trying to make people happy. It's a good thing he's charming and most people don't know what he's up to until it's too late, and by then they're happy about it because he was so charming in the process."

"Makes him a good front man, as long as you keep him in line." Marzie's face darkened again. "I used to think Jerry was charming, and he was, just in all the wrong way."

Cin laughed, doing her best to make it a joyful sound and not come across as snide in the face of Marzie's current situation. "I got no worries with Chad. He knows he's got a good thing, just like I have a good thing. He's not going to be off flirting when he's just trying to be charming."

"I hope you're right." Marzie's phone buzzed. She looked at the screen. "The county. I bet they're telling me you guys are getting the house and I'm getting nothing."

"Never know." Cin's phone rang with Chad's tone as Marzie answered her call.

"Hey, Babe, what's going on?" Cin answered Chad's call, since Marzie was taking hers.

"Thought you'd like to know we got the place. Jackson got the county to go for it. We go in this afternoon. Think RJ'll be available? I could use a little help, and would like to move quickly. Although we're focused on the house, we're also supposed to look for things in the yard too."

"I think Marzie and I are about done. I'll call him on my way back to the office."

"Great. See you at the house."

Cin frowned. "But I don't do demo, you know that."

"Yeah, but you can follow us around documenting things and holding evidence bags."

"Thanks, Dear." Although it wasn't how she'd planned on spending the day, Cin thought she might at least be able to get into the second story efficiency and see if there was anything up there that might say someone was still living in the place. There had to be some reason for the threshold.

Chad chuckled. "I love you."

"I love you too." Cin ended the call and set her phone on the table.

"Guess we can go back to the office and get you keys." Marzie ended her own call. "You got yourself a fixer upper, complete with skeletons in the back yard."

"Probably better than skeletons in the closet." As soon as the words slipped out, Cin wondered what else they were going to find at their latest project house.

# 9

The house was as dusty as it had been when they'd first looked at it. Part of Cin wanted a mask, but she hated them, so she opted to forgo. Chad insisted that everyone wear gloves, more to prevent fingerprints on potential evidence than to keep their hands clean.

"Okay, Cin's here to document everything we find," Chad said as they entered the house. "Cin, we're going to need pictures and a written record of things. RJ, as we find stuff, we're going to have to wait for her before we even dust things off."

Cin stared at him. "Okay, Chad. How are we going to know if something is evidence if it's covered in dust? I mean in some spots this dust is several inches think."

Chad paused and rubbed his beard-covered chin. "Good point. We're really not going to know if… say a knife has blood on it before we uncover it. I guess it's a good thing I brought the leaf blower from the house."

"I'm going to be outside if you're going to start blowing this dust around. It'll be like a sandstorm in here." Cin turned and headed toward the door.

"You know. I've only got one leaf blower. Why don't you and RJ look around the back yard, or go check out the efficiency?"

## Second-Story Hex

"I like that idea better." RJ turned around in the center of the living room and looked toward the door. "The big question I have, is if you're using a leaf blower, aren't you worried about losing something like hair samples or papers?"

Chad shook his head. "Nope. I'll be using it on low."

Cin rolled her eyes. There were times when her dear husband was just another guy... not thinking things through. Sure the leaf blower would move the dust around, but it had the potential for a lot of chaos. If Chad came out with too much dust on him, she was going to make him walk home instead of coating the inside of the car with dirt.

They all headed back out the front door. Chad was going to retrieve the leaf blower, and Cin and RJ wanted to be away from the waves of fine sand when Chad fired the thing up.

"Do you want to start in the efficiency or the yard?" Cin asked.

RJ shrugged. "You're the boss. I figure we've gotta go over both."

"Efficiency it is." Cin started toward the stairs that would take them up to the add-on. She'd felt the threshold again when they walked into the house. There was still no good explanation for it. Something was going on, and she doubted it was just Marzie being cursed. Being more open to odd things, she couldn't deny the energy of the place was off, unfortunately she couldn't figure out exactly how.

As they walked up the stairs, she checked the keys Marzie had given her. Other than being a brass color, the key for the efficiency was identical to the front door key. The dust on the stairs held just a couple of footprints. From the looks of them, they were Chad's familiar work boot and Marzie's heels. The two who'd made it the closest to the door before Chad had smelled the bones in the back yard.

The coroner's team hadn't bothered to fill in the hole

where they'd found the skeletons. It was a gaping wound in the greening grass of the yard. They'd have to get a team in with a tractor to back fill the hole and replant some of the grass in hopes the yard would look somewhat normal when it came time to rent the place. There was a lot to do before they got to that point, but it never hurt to start planning what needed to happen.

Cin paused as she looked at the hole. There was a pattern in the grass. She hurried up to the landing and stared out over the yard.

"What's up?" RJ asked a few steps behind her. "Not another body?"

"I don't think so." Cin pulled out her phone and started getting pictures of the pattern in the grass. "What do you see there?"

RJ shielded his eyes from the sun that was nearly directly overhead. "Hmmm. Kinda looks like a spiral, or maybe a labyrinth."

Cin nodded. She didn't recall feeling anything when they had walked out to where Chad said the bodies were. Even if the pattern wasn't visible from the ground, at least not with the barest of short spring grass, if it was magical in nature there should've been a feeling to it. Walking through the paths the wrong way should've triggered some kind of sensation, but there hadn't been anything. Finishing getting a few more shots from the landing, Cin slipped her phone back into her jeans pocket. Maybe her mother would have some insight on the pattern.

Slipping the key into the deadbolt, Cin opened herself up a little more as she turned the key. Nothing out of the ordinary. She touched the doorknob. It was warm to the touch, but the days were starting to warm quickly. As she slowly turned the doorknob, she held her breath.

The door opened. Nothing. The barest whisper of a threshold, nothing like the front door.

In the distance the leaf blower roared.

## Second-Story Hex

Letting out the breath she'd been holding, Cin forced herself to walk into the space.

She made it two steps, and the threshold that was missing at the door hit her hard in the face. Feeling her nose to make sure it wasn't broken, Cin staggered back a couple of steps. "Okay, somebody definitely still lives here."

"With all the dust?" RJ slipped passed her, seemingly unfazed by the threshold.

Pushing her sensitivity to paraenergy down, Cin stepped through the threshold without feeling it smack her hard. The place was as dusty as the downstairs was, if not more-so. It was small, barely large enough for a true efficiency, although there was a sink and a mini fridge that looked old enough to have been the first model of its kind to be released.

A brown curtain partitioned off the room from a toilet and shower. When RJ pushed it aside, the cloud of dust that swirled around him must have been close to what Chad was whipping up with the leaf blower downstairs.

RJ coughed and fanned the swirling dirt away from his face. "Can't say as I've ever seen this much dust in my life."

Cin had to laugh. "A sure sign you're new to the valley. Dust is a way of life around here. You might even start thinking it's the thing that holds the universe together."

"We had what I always thought of as plenty of dust back along the Front Range—" RJ stopped fanning the dirt away "—but this is just extreme. Still surprised this place isn't a complete desert."

"According to all the climate change theories, it will be in a few more years." Cin turned her attention from the microbath and looked around the rest of the space.

"It would be nice if they're wrong, but I can definitely tell things are changing. We're not having the winters we used to have in the eighties. I was just starting to get used to snow in feet, several times a year and then it backs down to inches." RJ shook his head. "Too fast for my taste."

"Mine too." Cin stared at the couch that looked to be in good shape, other than the inches of fine brown sand that covered it. It didn't make sense that someone had just deserted the place. Of course the skeletons in the backyard suggested it might not have been a simple desertion. The thresholds also said that there was something more going on.

A small wooden end table next to the couch was the only thing in the room not covered in years of dust. Cin stared at it for a moment. "Okay. This is odd." Chad wanted things documented, if it was something magical, they could decide later if they would show those pictures to the sheriff or not. Jackson wanted physical clues and the clean table wasn't exactly a clue to who killed the skeletons in the yard.

"Looks fairly new," RJ added. "Only thing in here that isn't covered, but there's no way someone could've put that in here without disturbing the dust."

Cin nodded. "Exactly."

She squatted in front of the table, and opened herself up a little more. The table's dark wood seemed to shine slightly in the afternoon sun coming through the sheers in the window. The curtains were yellowed enough to change the light coming in to a dull gold. Somehow the light around the table was more pure and perfect. It almost looked like there should be things sitting on the table. Ghosts of candles, crystals and books shimmered in and out of the light. Cin carefully reached for the table. A protective field radiated out from the table. She touched it and it burst like a soap bubble.

"I didn't mean to do that." Cin rocked back on her heels and stared at the table. The ghostly vestiges of pillar candles, crystals, and more vanished with it.

"That was odd." RJ stood quietly, guardian like a couple feet away. "Do you think that it might've been an altar at one time?"

Cin looked back over her shoulder. "What do you know of altars?"

RJ shrugged. "Not a ton. I sometimes help AJ with some of his research and when he was working on a paranormal romance series a couple of years ago, we did a lot of digging into occult stuff. This has all the earmarks of some kind of magical altar." He looked toward the window that showed the backyard. "If the grass patterning is some sort of labyrinth or something, makes me wonder if the bodies were part of a ritual sacrifice."

That was exactly what Cin was starting to think. "You mentioned your husband before. AJ. So he's a writer who does paranormal romances?"

"Actually he does all sorts of things. He's got so many ideas, he stays busy and makes a great living at it."

Although it was a slight deviation from trying to find clues, Cin wanted to know more about their new handyman who her mother said had the glow of magic. "Anything I might've read? What's his pen name?"

RJ laughed. "Which one? Like I said he has lots of ideas across multiple genres so he writes under several pen names. Most of his stuff is under AJ Hawkins."

Cin straightened and stared at RJ. "Wait a minute. AJ Hawkins, the New York Times bestselling writer of the Front Range Witch series, that is currently being made into a Netflix show, is your husband?" Cin was suddenly wondering even more about RJ and why he was out doing handyman work.

"Yeah, that's him." RJ darkened a bit. "Look, can we keep that all quiet for a bit. We came to Cottonwood to get a bit of a new start. Sure we're going to let everyone in town know in a while, but we want to make new friends without that hanging over us. To a lot of people AJ's a bit of a celebrity, and we're not here for that. We're here to just be us."

"Warts and all." Cin nodded. "I get it. But you should probably know, the gossip engine in this small town is powerful. I'm not going to tell on you, nor will Chad, but folks are always looking for something or someone new to talk about and you guys are ripe for lots of chatter."

"Thanks. We were kind of expecting that, but like I said, we just want to meet folks here as RJ and AJ for as long as possible." RJ turned back to the end table. "And maybe some of our research into weird can help with this."

"Maybe." Cin wondered how freaked out RJ was going to be when he found out their secrets. Being a witch married to a werewolf with two witchy kids and a motherly ghost were a bit stranger than just having a superstar author husband. "Right now, Chad and I are open to just about anything at this point, particularly with things getting weirder by the second."

As if on cue, Cin's phone rang with Chad's tone. As she pulled the phone out of her jeans, she frowned. Why was Chad being lazy and calling her instead of coming and getting her? As she went to accept the phone, she realized the she couldn't hear the leaf blower any longer, and hadn't since she'd been talking to RJ. "What's up, hon?"

"I think I need a little help down here. I set something off." Then the phone went dead.

# 10

Cin didn't even pause as she ran through the front door. RJ was just a couple steps behind her. The cloud of dust was settling. "Chad, where are you?"

"Back in the main bedroom!" A hint of nervousness colored his return shout.

She skidded to a stop as she entered the open French doors that went into the large master bedroom. The dust had been moved around and there was a large glowing cage around Chad.

"What did you do?" Cin walked in carefully, not wanting to accidently set off another trap that might be waiting for her.

"I don't know." Chad spread his hands in a gesture of innocence. "I was running the leaf blower and then all of a sudden, this thing sprang up around me."

Cin slowly walked around the cage. The bars were glowing red, looking like laser beams or something similar. She'd never seen anything like it.

"Magical cage." RJ stood in the doorway. "Why didn't it go off the other day when we were in here?"

"That's right." Cin pointed at the cage that was perfectly between the bed and the closet. "It didn't go off the other day when we were in the house with Marzie, so why go off now?" She didn't like Chad being locked up like some kind of animal in the middle of the bedroom, but had to stay calm and think their way out of the situation.

"Chad didn't come into the bedroom," RJ said. "That was just you, me and the real estate gal, what was her name? She was here before we got here. Could she have disarmed it for a little while."

"Marzie." Cin took a moment to think back and RJ was right. Chad had been checking the breaker box just outside the bedroom, in the closet with the water heater and forced air unit. "You're right, Chad didn't come in. I don't think she could've done anything magical." Marzie was about as normal as a person could get, at least as far as Cin knew.

"So this is a trap for what? A guy with a leaf blower?" RJ walked around the trap, his forehead etched with thought. "There's got to be a reason why it went off for Chad and not the rest of us, unless whoever set this was worried about handsome men coming after their wives."

"You think he's handsome?" Cin knelt on the blue shag carpet and tried to study the edge of the cage.

"Taking the fifth. He's my boss, and we're both married, so it doesn't matter." RJ chuckled softly and pulled over a chair from the side of the bed and climbed up to study the top of the cage that seemed to go up into the popcorn ceiling.

"Oh, we're going to be friends." Cin ran her finger through the carpet, but couldn't seem to find anything that would suggest an actual boundary to the cage. "I'm used to my friends thinking my husband's hot. He was one of the best catches in Cottonwood when we got married, and since he's losing weight, he'd on his way back to reclaim his title."

"And he's right here listening to you two," Chad mumbled. "What do you mean reclaim my title? You think I lost my hotness?"

Cin grinned up at him. "Not to me, hon, but let's face it, a lot more ladies and guys are watching you walk by since your bodily transformation."

"Thanks, Love." Chad smiled warmly down at her.

"Ah, if this cage thing is turning you two on and you need a minute or five, let me know and I'll go sort tools in my truck or something." RJ looked down at them from his chair. "I think I saw a grape around back that could probably use a nice conversation about now."

Chad looked up at RJ. "You talk to plants?"

"You don't? All plants could use a few words of encouragement from time to time. Helps them grow better." RJ shook his head. "If this thing has a roof, it's not in this room."

"I was just starting to think the same thing down here." Cin coughed a bit as a puff of dust rose when she put her hand down a little harder than she planned. The shag carpet was just gross and would be one of the first things she had RJ and the demo crew rip out.

"Maybe if we can figure out why it went off, we can deduce where the magical tripwire is." RJ jumped off the chair, sending more dirt rolling up around him.

Cin sighed. She and RJ had been sharing RJ's secrets minutes earlier; she couldn't see any way to avoid spilling their beans as well. With a glance at Chad for silent permission, she decided it was for the best.

As Chad let out a long breath, he nodded.

Returning it, Cin launched into the short version. "It probably reacted to him being a werewolf."

RJ's eyes grew a little wide and he cocked his head. "Hmmm. I'd almost say too short for a werewolf, but they do come in all sizes. Most of them tend to be on the fit side. I thought your jump the other day was more than just yoga."

Cin's jaw dropped. "Wait a minute. You said you knew about magical stuff due to research, don't tell me the same holds for werewolves."

"Yeah." RJ nodded. "During the early stages of writing

Front Range Witches, AJ and I managed to get an audience with one of the alphas in Denver. Really nice guy. He liked the idea of AJ's books being as authentic as possible, so as long as we don't go around telling everyone that werewolves are real, he was cool with AJ using him as a reference for the books. Tons of great info."

Chad looked confused. "Okay. I'm missing something here. Are you saying that RJ's husband is AJ Hawkings, New York Times Best Selling author of the Front Range Witches books? I always thought those were a little too spot on to just be fiction."

"You've read those?" Cin and RJ asked at the same time.

"Sure." Chad shrugged. "I do tons of miles every year between properties and conferences. You know I listen to a lot of audio books."

"Yeah, I figured they were work reference books," Cin said, trying to understand her husband's reveal of listening to steamy paranormal romances.

"All work and no play." Chad chuckled. "Gotta have a little light listening sometimes. Plus those finance books are a great way to fall asleep while driving and go off a cliff. I might survive, but if I wreck the car, you'll be mad, and we'd have a hard time explaining why I made it out alive and the car is a crumpled piece of scrap."

"Good point." Not caring about the mess she was going to make of her jeans, they were work clothes anyway, Cin settled on the rug. "Now, that does make a little more sense, it was set to catch magical creatures, but how do we disarm it?"

Chad screwed up his face. "I can't actually believe I'm suggesting this, but why not ask your mother?"

"Good idea." Cin stood, then looked at RJ. "So the rest of the family secrets are that I'm a witch and my dead mother still haunts us."

"Haunts, that's exactly what she does." Chad waggled

his finger toward the ceiling. "I hope you're on good terms with your mother in-law, and or that she's not a witch, 'cause if not, on either count, she won't leave you and your family alone… ever."

"AJ's mother loved me before she died." RJ laughed as he dusted off his jeans. "And so far, we haven't seen any sign of a ghost. Why don't I go down into the basement and see if there's anything down there that might be powering this? We might get lucky."

"Right now, we need some luck." Cin looked at Chad; if he was suggesting they call in her mother, who'd said previously that she couldn't cross the threshold, he was more scared of being in the cage than he was letting on. "I'll call Mom and see if she has some ideas."

RJ walked past her. "I think I recall stairs down into the basement in the kitchen, or just off the kitchen."

"I think you're right." Cin headed toward the front door. Since her mother couldn't cross the threshold the last time she tried, she was going to see about making sure there wasn't a problem, since they needed her help.

She stepped out onto the front porch, careful where she stepped since she didn't trust the porch to not disintegrate beneath her feet. Out of habit, she glanced around, making sure no one was watching. She wasn't in the mood to explain standing on a porch, shouting to a passerby.

"Mother, if you can hear me, I could use a hand." She was careful to project her words as well as she could. Words could carry out into the world and beyond when the speaker did it the right way.

After nearly a minute, she drew another breath to call again when her mother materialized in front of her. One second there was nothing, then there was a bit of colored haze that slowly resolved into the form of her mother.

"What can I help with, Cin?"

Cin looked around. "I take it you haven't been

following us around today."

Her mother laughed. "Sweetie, I know it seems like either with you or one of the girls all the time, but that isn't true. I do have an afterlife of my own." Then she put her hands over her ears. "We need to get that alarm turned off."

"What alarm?" Not being able to hear the alarm, Cin just pointed at the house. "Chad's stuck in a magical cage and we need to figure out what to do."

"You're going to need to invite me in." Her mother glanced around the porch and frowned. "I can't get past the threshold without an invite."

"I always thought that was for vampires, not spirits," Cin said.

"Sometimes humans get the rules screwed up, you know that." Her mother put her hands on her hips. "One vampire ghost gets caught needing help across a threshold and everyone jumps to the conclusion it was because he was a vampire, not a ghost."

"So it's reversed?"

"No." Her mother shook her head and sounded a little put out. "It's actually all of us. Vampires, spirits, the fae, most magical creatures. Weres aren't affected because they have a larger human aspect. Now are you going to go back into the house and invite me in, or not?"

"Oh. Yeah." Cin walked back into the house, stopping just inside the threshold. "Chasity Fisher, as rightful owner of this home, I hereby invite you in. Come in peace."

Her mother strolled in. "So formal. I guess I taught you well, didn't I?"

"Guess so." Cin turned toward the bedroom. "He's in here."

A look of disgust distorted her mother's features. "Seriously, we need to do something about that alarm. I'm not going to be able to do anything while it's going off, and who knows what's going to hear it and come running."

Cin shook her head and opened herself as far as she

dared. There wasn't anything registering on her senses. "Not hearing an alarm here."

"Must be on the spirit plane." Her mother frowned. "That still isn't good."

RJ appeared out of the kitchen. "I think I found something down there. Getting a hammer." He stopped halfway through the living room. "Oh, you must be Cin's mother. Hi. I'm RJ."

A warm smile chased her mother's frown away. "Charity Fisher. Yes, I'm Cin's mom. I'm glad she's finally hiring people with a bit of magic to them. "

Ignoring her mother's jib, Cin looked at RJ. "Hammer?"

"Yeah. Wait there and you can check it out with me. Maybe one of you two can double-check things before I take it apart. I'd hate to make things worse for Chad." Then he hurried out of the house.

"You know, it might be useful to take some notes as he disassembles this trap." Cin's mother looked down at the dust. She was the first one through the house that didn't disturb any of it. "This place is filthy."

"No one's lived here in years." Cin countered. "We'll have it cleaned up in no time."

"I don't even know why there are spirits living here."

Cin perked up and looked at her mother. "Spirits? We've got spirits living in the house? Is that why the threshold is still up?"

Her mother shook her head. "No. Spirits don't create a threshold. There's something more here than just that. It's probably going to be a long time before spirits come back anyway. All this noise is atrocious."

It would've been too easy to have her mother walk in and sort everything out for her. Cin knew there had to be some kind of answer; she just hadn't stumbled on it yet.

RJ reappeared with a yellow handled claw hammer.

"Okay. Come see what you think. I'm pretty sure this is the base of the cage trap." Without waiting for either of them to respond, he headed on down to the basement, hammer in hand.

Cin followed, when she reached the basement, her mother was already there, floating several feet off the floor, staring at an arrangement of softly glowing crystals held by wire and nails to the basement ceiling, which was the bedroom floor.

"Okay, that looks complex." Cin stared up at the strange crystals and symbols above her. It was an intricate magical circle. The crystals marked out the points of the pentagram. Runes decorated the insides of the points of the star. Some of the runes were glowing, and some weren't.

"Oh, my." Her mother drifted a little away from the circle.

"What is it?" Cin looked from her mother to the circle on the ceiling.

"That was set for anything that wasn't human or witch. Fae, spirits, vampires, werewolves, anything could've been caught by that trap." Her mother crossed her arms and glared at it. "A nasty piece of work."

"Do the glowing runes indicate that it's caught a werewolf?" Cin pulled out her phone and started clicking off pictures.

After getting no reply, she glanced over at her mother who had turned her glare from the circle to Cin.

"Well?"

"I should tell you to go study, that I'm not your ectoplasmic library. I left you all those books for a reason."

"And I've been going through things as I get time." There were times her mother didn't totally understand the busy modern life she and Chad lived. If she had three or four more hours in the day, she might get more studying done, as it was, she went looking for things when she needed them, and not before.

A lough huff escaped her mother. "Yes, the glowing ones are telling you what you caught in the trap, and in this case it's a werewolf."

Cin made sure to get a couple closer pictures of the glowing runes. "Thanks." Then she stepped back. "RJ, let's see if we can take this down without shattering any of the crystals. I want to take those home."

"You think they might be some of the evidence we're supposed to be looking for?" He gripped the hammer and moved a folding ladder over under the circle.

Not bothering to ask where he found the ladder, since the basement had a large assortment of shelves and other storage, Cin shrugged. "Not sure that's the kind of evidence the sheriff is looking for. Jackson and his deputies aren't prepared to deal with the supernatural."

"Which is why we're around," her mother added.

RJ went up the ladder and studied the circle for a moment, deciding where to start.

Cin pointed to one crystal, hoping she was right and it was the north one. "Start there. Then go counter clockwise to safely dispel the circle and hopefully the cage." She was a little surprised that the red glow from the cage didn't extend into the basement.

"Okay. You're the boss." RJ slipped the claws of the hammer under the wire and nail holding the crystal to the ceiling and started to pry it off.

The magic of the circle pulsed.

"Whatever you're doing stop!" Chad shouted from the bedroom. He stomped on the floor, sending dust cascading around them.

Her mother grabbed her ears. "The alarm just got worse."

"Don't do anything." Cin rushed out of the basement and to the bedroom. She wouldn't be able to live with herself if they'd done something that hurt Chad.

**67**

# 11

When Cin skidded to a stop with a cloud of dust in the bedroom, the magical cage was half the size it had been previously. The top of it was only inches from Chad's head. "What happened?"

Chad glanced up at the top of the cage. "I'm going to make a guess and say the cage didn't like you messing with its magic."

Cin frowned and shook her head. "It's not sentient. Not possible." At least she was fairly sure it wasn't possible. Magical traps weren't like modern home security systems that had an AI supporting them. They were literally simple constructs that had triggers and releases. It didn't make any sense that it would've picked up on RJ's tampering with it and then try and squish Chad. There had to be another answer.

"Yeah, this isn't good." RJ hurried into the room.

"I'm not going in there," Cin's mother called from the living room.

"Okay, taking this thing apart from downstairs isn't going to work." Cin glanced up at the ceiling. "Is there an attic in this place?"

RJ followed her gaze. "Guess we can look around. I don't recall stairs for it. The only up-going stairs I remember are the ones for the efficiency."

"And we didn't see anything up there that could be powering this thing, and it's not right over the bedroom. It's more over the kitchen and back bedrooms." Cin hmmed thoughtfully tried to think of everything they knew about the layout of the house. There had to be something they'd missed, she just wasn't sure what it was.

"I'll look around and see what I can find." RJ disappeared.

"Think you might give me a hand?" His voice came from the living room, he must've been talking to her mother. "There might be something hidden that I can't spot."

A hidden stairway and attic. Although Cin loved the idea of having such things in her own home, she didn't see how helpful it would be in either a rental or a flipper.

"An attic is extra space, we can get more for it." Chad eased down into a cross-legged stance, although his knees were so close to the bars that the glow near them brightened.

"We can't get anything for this place if we don't dismantle this trap and get you out." Cin pushed back at the beginnings of panic that were threatening her. She'd never dreamed they'd stumble onto a magical trap set for werewolves and other non-humans in a house they were trying to flip. What kind of people were the Stones and what kind of friends and enemies did they have? Every time they visited the house, they ended up with more questions.

"I trust you, your mother, and RJ to sort this out." Chad looked like he was about to reach through the bars to her, but the bars flared as his fingers approached and he jerked his hand back.

"We're going to do our best." Cin took a deep breath, trying to center herself. Would she ever be able to let Chad check out another house without her in tow, just in case more people had such traps set up, waiting for him or someone else to stumble into them?

RJ came back in the room. "Nothing in the way of an attic. I'm going to get a ladder out of the basement and check the roof. Who knows, maybe there's something up there."

"If not, you're going to have to take that circle apart as fast as you can," Chad said. "I'm a werewolf. I can survive a lot of things."

Cin shook her head and wanted to curse the magical cage that kept her from touching her husband. "Not magic. It's one of the things that can hurt you, a lot. We'll figure out how to take this down without hurting you."

If she stayed there with Chad in the cage she was going to keep worrying about it. "RJ, I'm going to come with you and hold the ladder."

RJ nodded. "AJ always fusses at me when I don't have someone holding ladders. It'll make me feel better too. Your mother can't hold things."

Cin's mother floated in the living room, a sure sign she was stressing. She normally kept her feet on the floor or ground, whatever the people around her were walking on. She said it made her feel a little more solid. "I'm going to go and see if I can find out anything more. That circle isn't something I've seen before."

"Okay. Don't take long." At times like that, Cin missed being able to hug her mother. She was holding it together fairly well, but a reassuring hug would have been great. "If you can run by the house and see if the girls are home, we might need a bit more help with this." It was a long shot, but maybe if the girls were with her, they could find a way to short out, or overpower the cage and then take it down.

Her mother drifted close and pressed her lips to Cin's cheek before vanishing. "Love you." The words seemed to hover in the air, fading more slowly than her mother had.

Cin let out a long breath. "Okay. Let's get that ladder and check out the roof."

Getting the ladder up from the basement was a bigger challenge than Cin expected. Even the calm RJ was cussing like a sailor by the time they found just the right angle to bring the ladder out into the kitchen.

RJ paused and wiped his brow with the back of his hand. "Okay. I honestly have no clue how they managed to get that down there in the first place."

"I vote we just leave it leaned up against the house when we're done." Cin took one end and carefully lifted it up so they didn't hit the kitchen table with it. "Okay, not up to the roof, just lying in the grass back there."

"I understand." RJ opened the backdoor and turned so they got the ladder out. "Now, do we know where on the roof we need to look?"

"Not in the back." Cin thought about the layout of the house. "Front corner."

"Over by the weathervane?"

Cin froze. There was a weathervane on the house. Stuck oddly near the corner. She'd never seen a weathervane positioned like that before. It had a huge metal crow on it. She'd spotted it when they first drove up. It had been what confirmed they were at the right house.

They reached the corner of the house and RJ extended the ladder out and leaned it against the house. He took a deep breath. "That's a steep roof, and like everything else, it's covered in dirt."

"The whole town's covered in dirt." Cin got a grip on the ladder as he started up to the roof. She glanced up. The metal crow on the weathervane looked down its beak at them, still seeming to be passing judgement on them. She suppressed a shiver.

RJ reached the roof, and slipped off the ladder like it was something he was used to doing every day. "Sorry for the dirt that's about to come down."

"Don't worry about it." Cin turned her face away from

the roof and looked at the ground as years of dirt and grit fell from the roof with each step RJ took along the steep incline.

A thick plume of dirt slid down right before RJ called down. "This is slicker than I thought it was going to be."

Cin shook out her hair and wished she'd thought to wear a hat. It was going to take a long shower to get all the grime out of her hair. And then, she was going to want a slow bubble bath. "Just don't fall."

"Doing my best." RJ scrambled a bit more, but the dirt cascading down missed Cin as he worked his way away from the ladder.

When the dirt stopped, Cin backed away from the ladder and looked up. RJ was just getting to the weathervane. The metal crow was spinning around like crazy, but the dust on the roof lay there like there was no wind at all. It was uncanny.

RJ crouched next to the vane, holding it with one hand to stop its frantic twirling. "Nothing exposed up here. Want me to take the vane down and see if someone thought to put something under it?"

One of the wonderful things about a lot of written spells was they could be covered up by something like the weathervane and as long as the writing didn't get smudged, it would be safely hidden away. Cin wouldn't mind if the judgmental crow never flew above the house again. "Sure. Go ahead."

"Going to have to pull a couple of shingles, but the roof will need to be redone anyway." RJ pulled his hammer from his belt loop and set to work.

Cin watched him work, wishing her mother would get back with some kind of new information that would help them get Chad out of the trap.

RJ got the weathervane free of the roof and knelt down. "Oh, yeah. Here we go."

"What is it?" Cin almost headed up the ladder to see for herself.

"Hold on." RJ held up his hand to stop her, then pulled out his phone. He took a couple of shots, then Cin's phone binged with a new message.

"That was easier." RJ called down

Cin pulled up the text and looked at the pictures of the roof. There was another circle. This one also had some crystals bound in wire similar to the one in the basement. The runes were also glowing in the same places as the other circle. Frowning. Cin studied the pictures. She couldn't be sure how to safely take down the circles without the magic killing Chad.

The air next to her shimmered and her mother appeared. "What did he find?"

"Another circle." Cin turned the phone toward her. "You?"

"We're going to have to dismantle the two circles at the same time. You'll have to take one and RJ will have to take down the other one. Piece by piece at exactly the same moment." Her mom glanced up toward RJ. "I might be able to carry messages back and forth."

"Or we can go into video chat." Cin looked up at RJ. "You can do video chat, right?"

RJ nodded. "Sure. AJ insists on staying up-to-date on tech."

"Good. I'm going to head down to the basement, and we'll do this together." She stopped at the porch steps. "Do you happen to have another hammer?" She hated feeling unprepared, and they were in her car and not Chad's if they'd brought Chad's he'd have had more tools than just the leaf blower.

Clutching her borrowed hammer, Cin made it up the stepladder and set the phone on the top of it. "Okay, start with the crystal you started with before." She was a little more comfortable on the stepladder than she would've been on the leaning ladder RJ had used to get to the roof.

"Got it." RJ held the phone with one hand, while slipping the hammer's claws under the wire and nail like he'd done before.

Realizing that she needed to finish getting that same crystal out of the arrangement, Cin mirrored the action. The nails popped out and Cin managed to catch the crystal as it fell, and somehow she did it without dropping the hammer.

"Chad, are you okay?" As she called out to him, she felt her heart pounding away. There hadn't been any flaring in the magic of the circle like there had been previously. She hoped he was alright.

"Good. Nothing changed though." The boards and shag carpet between them muffled his voice, but nothing had happened, and that gave Cin the confidence to continue.

"Okay, RJ, see the black crystal to the left of the one we just pulled?" Cin eased her hammer toward the nail and wires holding the next crystal in place.

"Yeah. That's next?"

"Yes. Tell me when you're ready?" She glanced down at the phone screen to see RJ getting his hammer in place.

"Let's do it." RJ nodded at the phone.

"Go." Cin pulled down on her hammer and the nail popped out easily. The wire unwound and dropped the crystal toward her. She grabbed it and put it next to the other one and the phone on the ladder.

"Chad?" She did her best to hide the nervousness tearing through her from her voice.

"All good."

She glanced at the phone. "Two down, four to go."

RJ nodded again. "Green crystal?"

"Green crystal." Cin wished she had time to wipe her sweaty hands on her jeans, but she wanted to get done and free Chad.

They moved in perfect unison and the nails came out,

the wire unwound and the crystal fell. Cin almost dropped it, but managed to keep it from hitting the ground. With a soft exhale, she placed it with the others.

"We're doing great." RJ said and gave her a shaky grin that told her he was as nervous as she was.

"Blue crystal next." Cin didn't want to congratulate themselves yet. There were still too many unknowns.

"On it." RJ got his hammer in place.

When they were ready, Cin yanked on the nail. It stuck. Chad screamed.

Cin threw all her weight into jerking the nail down and out of the circle of wire. The ladder wobbled and crashed under her. For a second she was suspended by the hammer and the nail, then the nail gave way. She fell to the basement floor and the blue crystal landed next to her shattering. One of the shards cut her cheek.

"Chad! Chad! Are you okay?" She was thankful the lights were still on. The only thing that could've made it any worse was if the lights had gone out.

"Hurry, Cin. Cage got smaller." His voice was rough and pained.

"I'm hurrying." She rolled to her feet, grabbed the hammer, and then struggled for a moment to get the ladder back up.

When she picked up the phone, RJ was staring at her through their connection. "What happened?"

"Nail hung. My end didn't come out as yours did." She felt stupid for not being strong enough to make the nail come out easily. It wasn't like she wasn't decent with a hammer. In some things, she was better than Chad. Sometimes a nail hung, but she would be willing to stress over every other nail she ever pulled or drove, if they could just get the last few out without a huge struggle. As much as she wanted to run up and make sure Chad was okay, she had to keep going. They had two more crystals to go.

The glowing in the runes started to flicker madly.

Cin hoped that meant the cage was losing power. It was hard to tell with magical spells. Some held together until the last piece of it was removed, and others were only as complete as the circle holding them together.

"Pink crystal," RJ said, as Cin got back on the ladder and set the phone back on its spot on the top.

"Right." Cin lifted the hammer to the nail. Her hands were sweatier than before. She griped the hammer as tight as she could. "Go."

The nail popped out easily and the pink crystal fell out and she caught it. As she placed it next to the phone on the top of the ladder, she glanced down. The other crystals weren't in immediate sight, she hoped she could find them when they were done. She wanted to check them out, try and study the magic. Although she never wanted to use something like that on Chad again, she never knew when someone else might cause trouble where the trap would come in handy.

"Last one?" RJ asked.

"Ready." Cin slipped the hammer's claws where they needed to be.

"Go." RJ said.

Cin jerked hard. The large clear crystal in the middle fell faster than the others had. She made a grab for it as the energy of the circle flared again. She lost her balance on the ladder and hit the floor hard. As darkness engulfed her, the sound of her mother calling her rang through her head.

# 12

"Cin, come on. You okay?" RJ stared down at her as he pressed a cool wet rag to her forehead.

"She's coming back around," her mother sounded more concerned than Cin had heard her being in years.

Cin wasn't sure if it she had a head injury or if her mother was passing in and out of RJ on purpose. Normally she hated it when people walked through her like she wasn't even there.

"What happened?" Cin moved slightly and her head throbbed horribly.

"Spell feedback, I think." Her mother hovered with her body slightly out of RJ's they looked like some odd double exposure. "At least you turned that damned alarm off."

"Chad?" Cin tried to get up on an elbow, but her head pounded. "Is Chad okay?"

RJ looked over his shoulder as something sounded on the stairs. It was lighter than Chad's footsteps should've been, but something was walking down the old wooden steps.

A huge black wolf came across the floor toward them.

"Define okay." RJ looked calmer than someone should, even if they'd had experience with werewolves before. There were few things more dangerous than a werewolf defending his mate.

"Oh, Gods. Chad. I'm sorry." Cin reached out for him. At least moving her hand didn't hurt like trying to move her head and rest of her body.

He nuzzled her hand. His fur was soft and soothing. After a moment, he lay down next to her, and put his head on her chest, holding her on the ground.

Cin had to admit it wasn't the most comfortable position. The basement floor wasn't hard concrete; it probably would've been a lot worse for her if it had been the case. Packed earth floors were hard enough, and she really wished she had something for the headache that seemed to be spreading.

RJ looked at her. "Do you want me to call 911? You might have a concussion. You fell off the later when the trap spell ended."

"Give me a couple of minutes. Do you happen to have anything for headaches in your truck?" Cin didn't like the idea of going to the ER. They could handle the cost, although it would make things tight when they didn't need them to be.

"I think there's something in the glove box. Might have a bottle of water too." RJ turned, stepped clear of her mother and headed up the stairs.

"He was a good choice for a helper," her mother said, once the door to the basement closed behind RJ.

Chad nodded as Cin stroked his silky head.

"I think so too. He's got a little exposure to things like werewolves."

"The girls are on their way," her mother said. "I am glad you didn't need their help for this. I know EEEK isn't ready, Char might be, but it might've been scary."

"I know." Cin had been scared, she couldn't imagine what the girls might've felt if they had to see their father trapped in a magical cage and then having that cage shrink around him. Although she wanted her girls to be ready magically for whatever they encountered, she was trying to keep the scary away from them for as long as possible.

Under her hand, Chad quivered and whined. He staggered a couple of steps away. Then he howled, it one of the saddest and most pained howls he'd ever uttered in her presence. The sound of bones popping and realigning made her want to cover her ears, but Cin didn't. Chad had to endure it, so she made herself do the same.

The basement door opened and RJ's footfalls came down the stairs, followed by two sets of lighter steps.

"Look who I fou-" RJ stopped mid sentence. "Girls, maybe you should wait upstairs."

"Dad—" Char sounded put out "—this is gross. Why did you have to wolf out? Geez. Did you at least not shred your clothes this time?"

Cin had to smile. "It's okay girls. He didn't have much of a choice."

"No clothes, sorry." Chad sat next to her and drew his legs up to his chest. He sounded exhausted, but then shifting always left him wiped out, and the farther from the full moon the worse it was. He had more control during the times the moon wasn't as much of an influence, but shifting wasn't easy.

"I think I've got something in the truck." RJ stopped and handed Chad a couple of bottles; one looked like a pill bottle and the other was water.

Looking up at him awkwardly from her prone position, Cin grinned. "Is there anything you don't have in that truck of yours?"

RJ smiled back at her. "A fair amount of things. I keep extra clothes in case I mess up something and don't have time to run home. Luckily Chad and I are fairly close to the same size. A little big is better than too tight. I'll be right back."

"Thanks." Chad opened the pill bottle and shook out a couple of capsules.

"No problem." RJ disappeared and hurried up the stairs.
Her mother nodded slowly. "Yes, keep that one."

"I think we have to now." Chad handed two pills to Cin.
"He knows our secrets and didn't totally freak out."

Cin and Chad hadn't told many of their friends about
Chad's attack. Sure most of the cops in town knew, but not
many of them had witnessed a shift. Other than a few of the
other witches in town, nobody knew about Cin and the girls.
It was hard keeping those details from the people around
them. It would be nice to have someone around they didn't
have to hide from.

"You're both right." Cin really wished the pounding in
her head would go away. Swallowing the pills hurt,
particularly lifting her head to do so. The water was
refreshing as it washed the capsules down.

"Wait a minute," Char had that put out tone that only a
teenage girl could have. "You told the new handyman
your…our family secrets. You're always going on about
how we have to not show off, and keep quiet about magic.
You know this guy for what, two days and you spill the
beans. How is that even close to fair?"

"Char." Cin forced herself to sit up a bit. "Sometimes
things get away from us. This house has some secrets, some
of them similar to our own. It was kinda hard not to let RJ
know about us, and he's a special case. Our rules are going
to stay in place."

"You know that's not fair." Char crossed her arms and
glared.

Chad cleared his throat. "No, Char, what's not fair is
attacking your mother when she's not feeling like defending
herself. We can talk about this later."

EEEK sighed dramatically. "It's always later. I'm with
Char on this."

The door above opened and RJ came down with a
couple pieces of clothing. "Not great, but at least you'll be
able to get home without drawing too much attention."

"You're great, RJ." Chad started to stand, then looked at their daughters. "Girls. And Charity." He made a twirling gesture.

"It's not like we haven't seen you after a change before, Dad." Char glared again, but turned.

Chad dressed quickly. RJ had a different style than Chad normally wore, but the red flannel shirt looked so good that Cin wondered if she could get him to buy a few and wear them when she wanted him to have a more rugged Colorado visage as opposed to his almost-preppy normal appearance.

When he was done, he offered Cin a hand up.

Cin grasped it. Like normal, when she took his hand, a spark of energy and excitement surged between them. It had been there the first time he'd touched her, and was still there after twenty years. She stood slowly, and still her head spun as she got to her feet. Keeping a tight hold on Chad, Cin closed her eyes and willed her head to stop and be steady enough for her to make it out of the basement and back to the sunlit afternoon outside. She'd had enough of the house with its skeletons and magical traps, at least for the day. She was more determined than ever to discover what the Stones had been up to, but she wanted to go spend some time in her bubble bath and recover from what she'd endured to that point.

She opened her eyes and everyone was staring at her.

"You okay, Dear?" her mother asked.

Cin nodded. The world turned again. "I think so. Going to take it slow."

"Let's get you home." Chad started toward the door.

"Girls, let's get home and get your mother some tea started." Her mother pointed up the stairs.

"Tea makes things better," EEEK said. "I'm glad you're okay, Mom."

"I will be." Cin took a deep breath.

The journey up the stairs was hard, but she made it. The fear of passing out and tumbling back down the basement stairs forced her to keep moving. With Chad and RJ behind her, the odds of making it all the way to the bottom were minimal, but she was determined.

"Let's wrap this up for the day," Chad said as they got out of the house. "We can go over more tomorrow. I'll let Sheriff Jackson know we didn't find anything interesting today."

"That's a bit of an understatement, but I bet the sheriff wouldn't understand about magical cages and stuff." RJ chuckled. "But yeah, I think I could use a bit of down time after nearly falling off the roof when that spell went off."

Cin stopped and grabbed his arm. "Wait, you almost fell off the roof? Why didn't you say anything about that?" She would've been hurt if their new friend had been injured or worse while helping them.

RJ waved her concern aside. "I caught myself before I went all the way down. I'm fine. Trust me, I've been in worse situations." He patted her hand. "I'm going to go relax, maybe get AJ to take me out for a steak."

Chad nodded. "A good steak sounds great right now."

"But we're not going out." Cin let go of RJ. "I'm not up for that. We're staying in tonight. See you tomorrow, RJ. Thanks for everything. I don't know what I would've done without you."

"Just glad I could be there." RJ patted her hand one more time and headed for his truck as the girls, in Char's Subaru, pulled out of the drive and pointed themselves toward town.

Cin sighed and leaned into Chad. "We got lucky today."

Chad kissed her cheek. "I know."

As RJ pulled out of the driveway, before Chad could get going, Sheriff Jackson pulled in behind them.

"What's going on?" Cin didn't want another major delay in getting home and chasing the stress of the day away.

## Second-Story Hex

"No idea, but I'm going to flip this house so fast it'll make the HGTV execs look slow if we can't get things done out here without Jackson coming in to check things out." Chad turned off the car and rested his hands on the steering wheel for a second before opening his door and getting out.

A momentary panic hit Cin, then she reminded herself that it wasn't a traffic stop. They were in the driveway of a house they owned. There wasn't an official reason they were aware of, unless Jackson had found out something about the skeletons, for the sheriff to stop them. With a quiet sigh, she leaned back against the headrest and let the guys talk as she closed her eyes.

She must've drifted off, 'cause she jumped slightly when Chad opened the door and got back in the car. "What was that about?"

Chad scratched his head, then glanced in the mirror before starting the car. "Not really sure. He said something about Lucille wanting him to come out and check on things. She had a feeling something was wrong."

"A feeling?" Cin glanced in the side mirror at the patrol truck backing out of the drive before turning down the road. She tried to think back on her couple of encounters with the iron force that was Lucille Jackson.

"Yeah." Chad started down the drive. "Guess you're not the only one around here that has feelings they have to follow."

"Guess so." If she hadn't been so tired, Cin would've given Lucille more thought, but her memories weren't all that firm about the woman. She could describe her, but little more. She was odd, but then a lot of people were odd and nothing to be worried about. With another sigh, she closed her eyes again, trusting on Chad to get them home in one piece.

# 13

The wind was up as Cin walked out the back of the house. They'd catalogued everything inside the place that could be considered either a personal artifact, or a potential clue. There were a lot of the previous and almost none of the later. Things like tooth and hair brushes had been put in Ziplock bags. Dirty laundry had also been bagged. All of those were things, Chad explained, that could hold DNA, even if it would be old and potentially damaged after years of exposure to the elements. Cin was tired of taking notes and pictures. She wondered how real CSIs managed to keep their sanity. Sure, she was a detail-oriented person, but there was too much minutia for her likes.

"Okay, let's check where they pulled the skeletons out, and then we can hand over everything to Jackson and call the scene completely closed and ready for demo." Chad strolled out across the lawn. He didn't act even slightly tired after three days of the small details of the house. If anything the amateur detective work was seeming to invigorate him.

"You don't think the coroner or the backhoe might've disrupted everything we could find here?" Cin followed him, totally lacking his enthusiasm for the job, other than the fact that the sooner they put a lid on the investigation, the sooner they could kick their remodel into full gear and get it done.

Poor RJ, who was going back over everything in the kitchen, looked to be as eager as she was to get their part of the job going.

"There's always the possibility they left something behind." Chad paused at the edge of the big hole in the yard and looked down into it. "See, there was one time that we had a buried body, this was early in my time on the force, and the only ID was a watch, but the coroner missed it since it fell off during excavation. We didn't find it until the third time we went over the scene."

"Honey, I really don't want to go over this place three times. One and we're good." Cin wanted to see sweat and new paint, not just the same little details over and over.

"I don't want to have to keep going over it either." He crouched for a moment before jumping down into the hole.

"Be careful." Cin looked down where Chad was using a small shovel he'd bought at the hardware store just for doing delicate excavation.

"Always." Chad glanced at each scoop of dirt before dropping it at his side.

Cin lowered herself down onto the torn-up dirt so she could watch him.

About an hour later, RJ came out of the kitchen and strolled over to Cin. "I think I'm done in the kitchen."

"Find anything interesting?" She knew they'd already been through the room.

RJ shook his head. "Not exactly, but I did notice something that's missing."

Hoping for something interesting, Cin straightened. "What?"

"It might be nothing, but it might be something. There's no salt." He shoved his hands into his pockets. "We're not sure the Stones were the ones into magic, but at this point, we're the only ones to pick up on any of it, or set any of it off."

"Right." Cin really didn't want to set any more of it off. Having Chad almost squished by the magical cage had been enough excitement for a while.

"Well, let's just say they were magical. Then where's the salt?"

"Salt?" Cin tried to look up at him, but the sun was too close to noon and reflected through his golden mane, momentarily blinding her as she caught a flash of his aura that was bright and large. She suddenly saw what her mother saw in RJ and resisted the urge to smile.

RJ nodded. His aura flashed as he did. "Right. What kind of magic users don't have salt in the house? At least every kind of magic I've help AJ research has had salt as a major component, particularly in purifications and binding."

Pursing her lips, Cin nodded back at him. She'd never known a witch to not have a large quantity of salt on hand at all times. RJ was right. The absence of it was as telling as if there had been too much of it. From the way the house looked, the Stones had simply gotten up and disappeared, maybe died. Their personal effects were still where they'd been in everyday life, including the small box of things like oils, herbs and stones that had been under the bed in the spare bedroom, which, when they looked at the arrangement of the several small tables around the space, had served as an altar room. She didn't remember seeing any salt in there either.

Cin glanced down into the hole. "What about you, Hon, any decent-sized bottles or bags of salt that you've found?"

Chad straightened and looked up at her. "Now that you mention it, no. But why would anyone take their salt? That's weird."

"Why were there skeletons in the back yard and a werewolf trap in the bedroom?" Cin shook her head, and when the skin on her neck complained about motion, realized she should've put sunscreen on. "This whole thing is weird."

"Yeah, you're right there." Chad bent back down and continued working.

"We can't tell Jackson there was salt missing and the Stones were witches and all witches should have salt in their cupboards." Cin sighed. "But thanks for pointing that out. Something else to think about. I wonder if the killer did some kind of cleansing ritual after the killing and took the salt with them."

"Good possibility," RJ replied. "Maybe they had done some kind of magic that required the circle to be up with the Stones, killed them during the ritual, and then used the salt for something to keep other people from sensing what they'd done."

"Or they scattered it when they buried the bodies." Chad held up a hand with some small, rough, white crystals reflecting sunlight. "I'd been wondering what this stuff was. It's not normal in the dirt around here."

"Another sign this was a ritual killing." Cin glanced back into the hole. A glimmer of light caught her attention. "What's that?" She pointed at it.

Chad turned and looked in its direction, but his shadow stopped the sparkle.

"Move to the side." Cin waved him to the left.

He did as she quested.

The sun reflected off something that looked like metal. It was in a slight white line of salt.

"This?" Chad reached down and tugged on a small chain. "Give me a second." He took the garden shovel and dug around the ends of the chain.

"Yes, that." Cin lay on the ground and looked over his shoulder. There was something about the chain that caught her attention and it was more than just something shiny glistening in the dirt.

"There's a charm of some sort on it." Chad still hadn't excavated all of it.

Cin pulled out her phone and clicked a couple of shots of the chain and the hole Chad was working on in the side of the skeleton's hole.

RJ leaned over next to Cin. "Charm. Be careful. Those things can be dangerous."

"Listen to RJ, hon. He's right about that, and you're not immune to magic."

"Yeah, I still have burn marks on my back from that stupid cage."

Cin had been putting salve on the marks for a couple of days. The long burns down his back were the first wounds he'd not healed during a shift since his attack. "It could've been a lot worse." She didn't like thinking about how close she'd come to losing him, all because of her slip in not being able to pull a nail. She didn't want him to take any more chances where magic was concerned.

"I lived through it. I've had worse." Chad got the chain free and held it up. It was a long necklace with a round charm on it.

Clicking off several pictures, Cin squinted at it. "Knock off some of the dirt, please."

Chad patted his pockets. "Do you have the paint brush?"

Cin thought there was something unusual in her back pocket and reached around to find the small paint brush there. "Okay, yeah I do." She pulled it out of her pocket and handed it to him.

"Thanks." Chad brushed the dirt off the medallion. It took several minutes to get all of it. Some of it was fairly deeply imbedded in the grooves and indentations.

When he held it back up, Cin's breath caught. "Yeah. Defiantly magical in origin." She clicked off a couple of pictures. "Let's see the back of it."

On the back of the charm was more runes and magical symbols. Cin peered at them, then took a couple of pictures of the back too. She pulled the phone close and zoomed in on the shots she'd taken. Some of the runes appeared to be Norse, but others were things she didn't recognize. "This is going to take some research."

"Then make sure your pictures are enough to do that from, cause this really should go to Jackson. It's the closest thing we've got to more evidence." Chad continued to hold it up.

"Looks almost like it was made with lost wax casting." RJ leaned a little closer to Cin, staring at her phone screen.

"Lost wax casting?" Cin reached down into the hole. "Let me see that."

Chad handed it up to her. "Careful of fingerprints. I don't want you implicated in this by a stupid mistake."

"Me either." Cin carefully held onto the chain that was fine enough to not take fingerprints. The lines were smooth, not rough. She'd seen some charms that had been scratched out on metal, normally brass or copper. The charm looked more like silver. It had been expertly crafted, and looked like with just a little effort it would be shiny again.

"Almost too good, isn't it?" RJ looked like he wanted to hold it and study it.

"Not amateur hour, that's for sure." Cin lay the necklace down and carefully took more pictures, making sure to get details of every rune and symbol there. From what she could tell, someone had use bits of several magical languages to craft the charm. It didn't tingle like active magic should, but that didn't mean it couldn't still be dangerous.

"Hey, there's another one here." Chad announced as he bent down and started moving more dirt.

"Are you positive?" Cin looked down at him.

Chad nodded. "There were two skeletons down here, why shouldn't there be two necklaces?"

Two necklaces. Two skeletons. Cin stared and wondered if they'd just found the murder weapon. Had years of being buried in the dirt rendered them inert? Was there still a possibility they might hold some magic she couldn't feel? Who knew the art of lost wax casting? She suddenly wanted to go visit various jewelry shops around Cottonwood and see if any of them had made the charms, or if any of them knew of a witch, or sorcerer who might be able to do that.

They dug around the hole for the rest of the afternoon without any further discoveries. Cin made sure to get good pictures so she could see about finding the meanings of the symbols, or possibly get the girls to do the research. It would be good for them. Remind them that magic wasn't always casting spells to find things. One thing she knew beyond a shadow of a doubt was that she didn't want her girls handling the charms. Even if they weren't the murder weapons, there was too much of a chance of things going wrong. The marks on Chad's back were the only injuries she wanted her family to suffer for gaining possession of the house. Sometimes cheap things ended up being way too expensive in the long run.

# 14

Cin stared at the design program without really seeing it. After spending the evening going over the runes and symbols they'd found on the charms, they weren't close to figuring out what the necklaces were for. Most of the markings had something to do with death. There had been thirteen of them on both sides of the charms, and the markings were different on each side. A total of twenty-six symbols and she hadn't been able to find all of them in her books. She was still short five symbols, and then also figuring out what it all meant when it was configured the way it was on the charms. With many magical symbols, like basic letters, there could be multiple meanings, determined by things on either side of them.

Sliding back from her desk, Cin rubbed her eyes and stood. She'd never been a big one on using charms like the ones they'd found. They screamed a level of high magic she'd only heard of in legends. Whoever crafted them was dangerous, and she really hoped they weren't still running around Cottonwood.

The front door opened and seconds later, Chad strolled into Cin's office. "How are you coming on the designs for the house?"

Cin shook her head. "Don't ask. What did Jackson have to say when you gave him the charms?"

"That was a little interesting. He looked a bit scared." Chad leaned against the doorframe and cocked his head. "I've been pondering that. He thanked me for finding them and was a little disappointed that we couldn't find anything the state forensics office could use to get DNA off of. They're still waiting to hear back from them about the skeletons' DNA, but it would be nice to have an easy tie to the house."

"I think easy is too much to ask on this one." Cin wandered over to the mini fridge in the corner of her office and pulled out a bottle of water. She pointed it at Chad, who shook his head, so she opened it and took a drink. "I mean, the Stones have been missing for what, ten years?"

Chad crossed his arms and nodded. "Thereabout. The cold cases are always the hardest ones to solve."

"Right. But honestly I'd like to figure this out before we get the house done so we can either rent it or sell it without worrying about the people who are going to move in there."

"That's one of the things I love about you." Chad straightened and walked over to take her in his arms. "You're always worrying about other people."

Cin leaned into him and enjoyed his warmth as he held her. "It's just who we are. We care." She included him in there, since she knew he worried about other people too. It was one of the reasons he'd become a police officer—to help other people, folks he might not know, but still worried about.

"And if we're going to keep caring about other people, we're going to have to have the money so people aren't worrying about us." Chad kissed her cheek and stepped away. "We need to figure out what we're going to do with that house. RJ's over getting the last of the dust and sand out. The Demo crew is cleared to get started tomorrow. We're going to need a plan to know what to do next week."

"Right." Cin stepped out of his arms. "I'm thinking about opening up that east side of the house. We'll lose that one odd bedroom, but if we go into the basement and finish it out, we can get another two bedrooms to make up for it. The walls aren't loadbearing, so knocking them out won't be a problem, and we can end up with a great room that runs from the front of the house all the way back."

Pursing his lips, Chad nodded. "So that would leave the master bedroom on the main floor, and then the basement would have two either guest or kid rooms."

"Yes." Cin pointed at him as she paced and thought. Moving around it was easier to not stop and think about the charm. "We might move the pantry, and that would give us a little more room to either expand the master bathroom, or add a closet where the pantry is now that could open into the bathroom."

Chad tapped his lips thoughtfully. "Two closets in the bathroom can be a nice selling point, and pantries aren't as big a thing as they were a few years ago."

"Exactly." Cin picked up her tablet from the desk and pulled up a blank doc for taking notes. She didn't want to lose any of the ideas. "For the moment, stay out of the second story efficiency. I think we'll want to look at either making it bigger, or at least expanding the bathroom to make it more appealing."

"If it's more than just an efficiency, it would rent for more."

"That's what I'm thinking too." Cin grinned. It was always great when they were on the same page. They often worked as a well-oiled machine, each playing off the other and coming up with some spectacular ideas. House flipping was still new enough, as was property management, that they hadn't fallen into any repetitive ruts. She knew other couples who'd tried working together and failed. Most of the time, Cin looked forward to years of working closely with Chad.

"And if we decide to sell, having a nice rental, or kids' suite could be a great selling point." Chad leaned over the desk, and picked up a style magazine. "What would you say about trying to do something cool that might get us mentioned in a magazine like this?"

"I'm not sure we're ready for something like that right

now, but it would be incredible." Cin returned to her chair. "I think we need to do a few places first, get awesome at it, and then plan something amazing."

"A great crew behind us will help us with that." Chad returned the magazine to the corner of her desk. "RJ's a good start at that crew."

"This sounds like you're thinking about flipping a lot more houses than renting them." Cin reached over and straightened the pile of magazines on the desk.

Chad shrugged. "Not totally sure. I've been trying to think long term. That means thinking now, and later. Later being rentals, but now means turning things around quickly so we can get more money to buy more places."

"So setting up a cycle of buying, remodeling, and reselling and rentals." Cin set her tablet down with her notes still on the screen. "That's going to mean thinking ahead. Keeping the properties we think will be in zones of growth and therefore places we can get more for, or be easier rentals."

Chad nodded. "Like the condos outside Wolf Creek. I wish we could find more deals like that."

"If we've got the money at the time, we can move quickly on the deal." Cin grinned. Sometimes focusing on the real world and grounding in things like finances helped her think. Taking a step aside was clearing.

Her immersion in the real world was interrupted by Chad's phone ringing with an incoming call. He glanced at the phone. "Jackson." Then he swiped it to answer. "Hello, Sheriff, how can I help you?" "Really?" "How is that possible?" "Do they think they're that old?" "Okay. Well that makes me feel better." "Yes, we're going to start demo tomorrow." "Thanks." He swiped off the call and slipped the phone back into his pocket.

"Don't keep me waiting." Cin stared at him.

"They couldn't get any DNA off the bones. They think they were too old."

Cin's eyes widened. "Too old? How is that even possible? They can get DNA off dinosaur bones. These were definitely human skeletons."

"Hard to say." Chad rubbed his chin. "Sometimes the DNA lab runs into problems if the specimens aren't preserved correctly."

"Really, would that problem be in the sheriff's office or the fact the bones were in the ground for years?" Cin was trying to figure out where to lay the blame for the lack of evidence. She wasn't sure what made her feel better, the fact that they couldn't ID the bodies, or if they'd turned out to be the Stones.

Chad shrugged. "Again, hard to say. Could be either, but since we're fairly sure that the bodies are recent, I'd lean toward it being a problem at the sheriff's office."

"Then they could like send them another bone or something?"

"Maybe, but probably not. The big problem here is that as far as anyone's been able to tell the Stones had no next of kin. Nobody has come forth to claim their property or look for them, or anything. That's why we were able to get the place so cheap."

Cin blew out a long breath. "And then we shouldn't look a gift horse in the mouth, just slap some new shoes on it and get it sold." She didn't like that feeling. There was magic afoot, potentially dangerous magic, and she wanted to dig deeper and figure out what was going on. Sure she could do that based on the charm and the crystals they had from the magical trap, but having people to connect to the magic would make her feel better.

With a bit of work, maybe she could track down the craftsman who had made the charms, then maybe she could figure out what they were made for. The combination of the salt in the grave, and the modern chain told her they weren't dealing with ancient bones. She had a pair of modern corpses and needed to find out who they were. All the planning on redoing the house wasn't going to help her stop worrying about the skeletons.

"I'm going to be there during demo."

Chad blinked and stared at her. "Hon, you hate demo. I know we haven't done much of it, but you've never done that before."

Cin sighed. "We've never demoed a witch house before. You're going to need me there in case there are more traps waiting. Unless the sheriff is incompetent, the only other option is that someone crafted something that could get rid of DNA." Her mother's phrasing, devoid of life, came back to her. DNA was the building blocks of life. The charms had erased those blocks from the skeletons. That was major magic.

"That shouldn't be possible." Chad frowned.

"Even ten years ago, it should've been impossible for two people to just disappear, but they did." An idea hit her and she put her tablet into her desk drawer. "I need to head out for a bit. I'll see you back at the house."

"Where are you going?"

Pulling her purse from the coat hook just inside her door, Cin grinned at him. "Going to talk to someone who's been around for years, and has the ability to glimpse into the future."

Chad shuddered. "Have fun with that."

"I'll tell her you said hi." Cin headed out of the office, hoping her destination wasn't going to be overly busy in the middle of the afternoon in the middle of the week. If she was really lucky, Kama was going to know she was coming and have the table and cards set up for her. Seeing the future wasn't something Cin or her mother were any good at, but she did have resources who were.

# 15

The parking lot of The Third Eye Open was free of cars as Cin pulled in and took a spot right next to the small adobe building. The sign above the door was a simple eye of Ra, but the larger, more prominent billboard was one of the largest in Cottonwood with huge script letters declaring the business name over a larger eye that many passersby claimed was watching them as they walked, biked, or drove past. As she glanced up at the sign above the building, Cin wasn't totally sure if the eye blinked or not.

Before she could touch the door, it swung open and Kama, the proprietress and chief seer, stood there smiling. "Cin, darling, it's been too long."

"Kama, you knew I was coming." Cin crossed the threshold, noting the tingle that most places of business didn't have, but then Kama and her family lived above and below the small shop.

"For days." Kama gave her a big hug. "It gave me time to properly brew us tea."

Cin didn't really want to know what kind of tea had to be brewed for days. She returned Kama's hug. "Then you know why I'm here."

"Always, my dear, always." Kama gestured back to a midsized table set for tea. The sterling tea set was sitting on a silver tray with steam rolling out of the pot's spout. There was enough candle light in the room to glisten off the matching silver teacups.

"You didn't have to make tea just for me." Cin came to Kama often enough to know where she was expected to sit at the table and took her customary seat.

Kama smiled and poured the tea. "I know, but it's so nice to sit and talk to another practitioner from time to time, even if you do come for business." She handed a teacup to Cin.

After accepting the tea, Cin sniffed it, enjoying the waft of herbs that came rolling out of the cup. In addition to being the best seer in southern Colorado, Kama made a mean pot of tea. Odds were, it would be empty before she left the shop. Cin and several other people had told Kama that if she ever wanted to get out of the fortune telling business, or just wanted a lucrative side hustle, she should open a teashop. She wouldn't compete with the coffee shop, which was strictly coffees. Since Cottonwood was growing, there was room for any new business that wanted to try its hand at the market.

"How have things been?" Cin knew they'd get around to what she needed when it was time. Kama wasn't to be rushed.

"We're between crowds." Kama sipped her tea. "The summer tourists will start soon, and the stars are saying it will be a good summer here in Cottonwood. The winter was good, particularly when the snows came. Travelers couldn't reach the slopes and had to have something to do before they turned around and went home."

Being at a crossroads made Cottonwood fairly unique in the busy Colorado mountain tourist areas. It was between ski slopes. The Great Sand Dune Park drew people in, as did the alligator farm, and the hopes of seeing UFOs. But the tourists were extremely seasonal, and when the weather turned, as it had several times during the winter, folks who had hopes of getting to the ski slopes found themselves stuck in the cold valley until the roads cleared. During those times all the shops in town did great business.

"I'm glad things went well for you this year. I've heard from other people that it was a good winter." Cin sipped the tea. As the warm liquid slid down her throat, it spread an easy, comfortable feeling through her core.

"Yes. I think the pot farms will bring people, but it won't last." Kama shook her head. "The water table is already taxed, and although the snows were enough to disrupt the travelers, that won't always be the case. The snows are getting smaller and smaller each year, and that will mean less and less water. The people with the green medicine will find it hard to survive here as the climate changes and this land finishes its transition to desert."

Cin chuckled. "I think we're almost there." The valley wasn't as green as it had been in her youth.

"You're right. The browning of death will spread over the valley in the coming years. We will find only along the river will be green." Kama closed her eyes and sighed. "This all makes me sad, but then seeing the future isn't always about revealing the sunny things people want to hear about." Kama set her tea down, looked at the pot before pouring herself more, then moving the tea service to the side of the table.

Familiar with Kama's routine, Cin knew their idle talk was over, and the fortuneteller was about to start.

Looking toward the ceiling, Kama ran her short fingers through her long, curly black hair that had just enough gray coming through to add sparkles in the candlelight. No one knew how old Kama was. She had been a Cottonwood staple for as long as Cin could remember, and even Cin's mother had come to Kama when she needed some guidance during uncertain times.

When Kama looked back toward the table, there was a deck of cards lying off to the side that Cin didn't remember seeing, nor had she felt any form of magic moving them around. Kama picked up the cards and began shuffling.

"There's an aura of death around you right now." Kama skillfully moved the cards from hand to hand. "There are secrets that you need guidance on."

Cin nodded slowly.

Kama fell silent as she shuffled the cards. The candlelight played off the rings on her hands, drawing Cin's attention and helping her drop into an almost trance-like state.

"Here, put some of your energy into the cards." Kama slid the cards over to Cin.

Blinking, Cin stared at the cards for a moment as the trance was broken. She picked up the cards that hummed with Kama's power. With practiced ease, she focused on the skeletons they'd found, the charms and magical trap. She wanted to know who had killed and then set the trap. Although she understood the cards wouldn't be able to name a killer directly, she hoped for clues that would lead them to something solid they could take to Sheriff Jackson.

"Careful." Kama laughed. "You might make my cards burst into flames with your intensity."

Cin stared at the large cards in her hands. They were glowing with her power. "Wow." She set the cards down on the table and quickly cut them into three stacks, then returned them to one deck. She couldn't remember doing that in the past.

"It happens sometimes." Kama reclaimed the cards. "You are worried about this. I think you are wanting to keep people safe. It is who you are."

"Yes." Cin nodded and watched as Kama gave the cards another quick shuffle.

Kama set the cards on the left side of the table and laid out the first card. She placed it on the table to her left, near Cin. It was a seated woman with a crescent moon behind her and a cat at her feet.

"You are always the priestess, my friend." Kama smiled. "It is good that some things never change."

Cin didn't say anything, letting Kama see what she saw as she laid out more cards.

## Second-Story Hex

A card with two people drinking from golden cups with a bright sun behind them went into the middle of the table.

Kama nodded. "A happy couple. A new home."

The next card went down above the central. A man lay on a bed with swords hanging on the wall above him.

"Sickness, something forgotten, or misplaced."

A dark card with a winged devil holding the chains of two people went below the other two. Kama pursed her lips and studied the layout for a moment. "A third party, an outside influence that encouraged decadence."

The card laid down to the left of the central card was a man swinging a staff around, fending off other, unseen opponents. "There was a history of minor violence, but nothing major."

To the right of the central card, she turned over a card with a silver skeleton walking through a field swinging a scythe. "It led to death."

Crossing the central card, she laid out a man who stood at a crosswalk holding a lantern. "It was just a passage." Kama tilted her head as if to see the cards better. "There's secrets trying to be hidden, but the light shall shine on them soon, and the devil will be revealed for who she is."

"She?" Cin broke her silence. "You're sure it's a she?"

Kama raised her hands. "As sure as I can be. There's a deep fog over your skeleton house."

Cin had been doing her best to not call the house their skeleton house, but in the back of her mind that was how she'd been thinking of it. That mindset was one of the biggest reasons she wanted to find out what had happened, lay the skeletons to a proper rest, and cleanse the property.

Not close to finished with the reading, Kama laid out a card with a man working hard on making pentacles that hung around him. "There's much work still to be done. Your men are strong and will do a good job." She looked at Cin and smiled. "It's always good to surround yourself with strong men. They will help protect you in dark times."

The next card which went above the hardworking man, was a bright sun with a running naked baby. "You want to make everyone happy. It takes a lot to diminish your light. Let the young ones help. It is good for you and them."

Cin resisted commenting how much she liked letting the girls help as long as it was safe to help. She wasn't about to do anything that put them in any kind of danger.

Above the Sun went its exact opposite. A full moon looked down on a stream with wolves on opposite sides howling. "The secrets worry you. Things will cycle and the dark will be exposed before it can eclipse the light."

Quickly she completed the spread with a regal looking man sitting on a horse holding a huge coin. "And money is running toward you." Kama chuckled. "That's is better than it running away from you." She leaned back in her chair and studied the throw.

Even though she wanted to start asking questions, Cin remained silent. It was proper to let the seer look over the entire picture she'd laid out and see what more came from seeing the cards spread before her and looking for their associations with each other.

Kama tapped the card of the moon. "Things will come to a head when the moonlight uncovers more secrets. Be careful near the moon."

If it was going to be during the full moon, she'd be watching out for Chad as well as trying to sort out their mystery. This was going to get complicated fast. Chad was always on edge during the days of the full moon, and they locked him in his wolf cave at night.

Pulling another card, Kama laid it over the base card. It was a woman sitting on a throne with a staff in her hand. "She's a hard woman, powerful, knowledgeable, dark hair. Dark magic." Kama frowned and pulled another card. A brilliant star shone above a man who poured water into a stream while putting one foot down in the water while the other stayed on the land. "She hides behind the stars. She thinks the stars make her safe."

Kama shivered and put her hands on the table. "We're looking too hard, too close."

A wave of magic washed over the shop. Candle flames flickered.

Cin shivered by the sudden cold that filled the place.

"No!" Kama pounded on the table and stood. "Take your darkness out of my shop. You are not welcome here."

The force of Kama's magic lashed out at the magical probing that had come toward them. She shoved it back out, and then with a tired huff, she plopped back into her chair. Quickly, she scattered the cards disrupting their vision before returning them to the deck.

Only after the cards were wrapped back in their silk bag did she turn her attention back to Cin. "She's trying to hide. We came close to seeing her and she's angry. Be careful of stars. She's hiding behind the stars."

The image of the man with one foot in the river and one on the land echoed in Cin's head. She tried to think of who she knew that matched that and would be considered a star. It didn't make much sense.

"Thanks, Kama. I'm sorry if I've drawn attention to you." Cin stood to leave.

Kama caught her hand. "Cin, dear, be careful, you're looking down dark tunnels to the past. Some things are best left buried. But it's too late for that now. Show her that everyone is accountable. If you have to, be a force of Karma."

Cin squeezed Kama's hand. "Thanks for the insight. If you feel anything else, please let me know."

"I will." Kama returned Cin's squeeze.

"Thanks for the tea. It was wonderful as always."

Kama smiled. "Next time, come just for tea and talk. It's the simple things that help us remember how to live in these busy times."

"That sounds wonderful." Cin gave Kama a parting grin before turning and leaving the shop.

Outside, everything looked the way it had when she'd gone in. There was no evidence they'd gotten a rise out of the magic user who had killed the skeletons, most likely the Stones. It was a nearly perfect spring day that held a promise of a hot summer. But sometime in the next ten days, things were going to come to a head. Since Chad's attack, she kept a calendar where she tracked the moon more closely than she ever had before. The time was limited to find out what had happened and become a force for karma. She never viewed herself like that before, and wasn't sure if she was ready to take on such a mantle.

# 16

The plume of dust rising out of the house reminded Cin why she didn't like demo days. She couldn't imagine what the place would look like if Chad hadn't spent hours with the leaf blower and windows opened wide to get a lot of the dust out before they started. After a brief discussion, they'd decided to let RJ and Chad handle most of the actual banging and pulling involved in demo, and had their crew hauling things out to the portable dumpster that was parked a few feet off the front porch steps to make it easier to carry the refuse out and throw away. Some of the furniture had gone in the dumpster, and a few pieces that were still in good repair were off to the side so the Arc could stop by and pick it up. Giving to people who needed it made Cin feel good. In tough times, a lot of people in Cottonwood relied on second-hand stores like the Arc and Goodwill to find things they needed without paying an arm and a leg for them, or having to drive to Pueblo or Denver.

Cin had marked a couple of areas, like the bathroom, for delicate destruction, wanting to keep some of the fixtures. Even if she didn't use them in rebuilding the house, there would be other projects down the road they'd be perfect for. She hated wasting something that might come in handy on another project.

"Hon, come look at this," Chad hollered from the bedroom.

A chill went through Cin as she hurried toward him. She didn't want to have a repeat of the magical cage that had caught him in that space before.

Chad knelt on the floor where the cage had been. The carpet and pad had been rolled back and was being hefted up by two of the demo crew who were taking it out to the dumpster. "Looks like what we found downstairs and on the roof."

Cin frowned as she looked at the markings on the particleboard floor. The dark magic marker symbols were identical to the other ones except that they didn't have wire and crystals; putting wire and crystals under the carpet would've made uncomfortable bumps that guests might have noticed.

She pulled out her phone and snapped shots of the markings. "Someone really wanted to make sure the cage spell worked right. Luckily, we were able disarm it. If they'd put the crystals and such from the basement under the carpet, we wouldn't have been able to."

"Do you think this means they wanted a way to make sure they could disarm it?" Chad rocked back on his heels and smiled, like he was trying to relax her. It didn't help much.

Cin shrugged and put her phone back in her jeans pocket. "I don't know. Possibly." She glanced up at the ceiling. "I wonder if there's another set of symbols under the popcorn."

"I guess we'll find out when we scrape that crap down. I really don't understand why people thought that was a good idea." Chad sighed.

"It was all the rage for a while. I think people thought it helped with soundproofing or insulation. But I'm thinking we might come in here and put some stained wood up there and it'll look nice." Cin pulled out a magic marker and set to defacing the magical symbol, just in case it flared up and gave them a problem.

"Found it!" RJ's voice rang out from the kitchen.

"What was he looking for?" Cin glanced at Chad as she straightened and returned the marker to her pocket.

"No clue, he was cleaning out the pantry." Chad followed her as they headed for the kitchen.

Most of the cabinets had already been pulled out, and the pantry door was wide open. The old fridge was at an angle, waiting for a couple of workers to take it out. The linoleum on the floor lay in a disorganized pile, also waiting to leave the building.

"What did you find?" Cin stopped just inside the pantry door.

"Their stash of salt." RJ stood where one of the sets of pantry shelves had swung out, revealing another set of shelves that were full of jars of herbs, resins, and all sorts of magical supplies.

"Wow." Cin's jaw dropped. "I've seen occult shops that don't have this good of a supply."

"Way out here, maybe they were afraid they'd need something and wouldn't have time to get it." Chad started toward the shelves and Cin put out a hand to stop him.

"We've already encountered one trap in this house, I need to check this out." Cin slipped past RJ. "You didn't do anything beyond open the door, did you?"

RJ shook his head. "Nope. Well, unless you count peeking in."

"Since you still have your eyesight, I guess you're safe there." She grinned.

Rubbing his eyes, RJ frowned. "Never thought of that."

"And luckily, most magic users don't think of such things either." Cin moved the hidden door a little wider.

"You're the lucky one." Her mother appeared in front of RJ. "Your mother thought to teach you about such things."

"Hi, Charity," RJ said.

"Such a nice young man." Cin's mother flashed him a tight smile. "I figured there would be at least one hidden room in this place." She placed a hand where the back of the movable shelf had been. "There's just places I can't get into here. And the walls seemed too thick."

Cin turned toward her mother. "And you didn't think to tell us about that before?"

Her mother shrugged. "Figured if I was just being a silly ghost, you'd work too hard to find nothing, and if I wasn't, you'd find it sooner or later. There is a magical shield here, like someone was, or is determined to keep spying spirits out."

Pausing before she picked up anything on the shelves, Cin looked back at her mother who was still outside the hidden pantry area. "Wait a minute. The trap spell had major physical components, so it would survive the death of the caster, but this house still has a threshold, and the shields to protect form prying eyes are still intact. There's no way those skeletons in the yard are the Stones."

"What do you mean?" Chad frowned and leaned against the pantry door.

"Spells and wards that don't have a physical component to them, that aren't designed to last forever, fade when the caster dies." Cin relaxed to the point where she could see the ward that kept her mother from the hidden space. The magic was thin and delicate, but still strong enough to block the ghost of a powerful witch from entering. "Either there's been someone here after the Stones were murdered, or those skeletons in the yard are their victims and the Stones left town after killing them and burying them back there." Even as she voiced her thoughts, Kama's reading a couple days earlier came back to her. There was something she was missing, beyond knowing exactly where the Stones were, and who the skeletons were. "Chad, when we get done here tonight, can I get you to run to the station and go through missing persons reports from back when the Stones disappeared?"

"After dinner, I'll see about logging into their system and doing it from the house." Chad dusted his hands on his jeans.

RJ turned and looked at him. "You can still do that?"

Grinning, Chad put a finger to his lips. "Small town departments run both faster and slower on some things than big towns do."

"Ah." RJ nodded slowly.

"Besides, doing it from home, I can have a beer and not have to deal with Harvey and some of the others asking me if I still chase cars."

"They do that?" RJ frowned. "That's mean, or juvenile."

Chad waved the comment away. "Not exactly. High stress jobs you get a warped sense of humor. If it were anyone but cops, I'd say you were right, but gallows and junior high humor is the way cops operate."

"It takes some getting used to," Cin added. "Guess you were never in the service."

RJ nodded again. "Yeah. My dad had a handyman business for years. I just fell into that and repairing electronics. When I met AJ, I was his personal assistant until he outgrew my ability to keep up with and we had to hire that out. Now I do this to keep my mind busy. You guys are a lot more fun than just playing video games all day long."

Cin laughed. "I'm glad."

"Could you take down this ward already so I can go through this selection?" Her mother asked. "You're on the inside of it, shouldn't be too hard."

"Okay." Cin put her hand against the ward. She closed her eyes and drew energy from her personal reserves, then pushed it out into the magical wall. It shimmered for a moment, then fell.

"Thank you." Her mother walked through her and started studying the shelves. "Whoever put this collection together was definitely working with several kinds of magic. There are things in here that are only used in high magic, some used in shamanic rituals, and nearly everything for basic Wiccan stuff."

"Sounds like the symbols we've been finding and the work on that charm." Cin looked over her mother's semi-transparent shoulder. "Doesn't really help us figure out who these belonged to."

"That on its own doesn't, but look at these labels, dear." Her mother pointed to the closest bottle, a jar of chamomile flowers. "The labels are handwritten. You just need to match the writing and you'll have something."

Although she wasn't sure where she'd get samples of people's handwriting, Cin had the urge to hug her mother. It was the first concrete clue they had. If they could go through old records, they might be able to match the writing. She paused. "That's what's been missing this whole time."

Chad cocked his head and stared at her. "What?"

"Writing. When we went through the house looking for clues. There were hair brushes, tooth brushes and things like that. But there's not been a family bible, love letters, holiday cards, or things like that. It's like someone came in and removed all that but didn't bother with things that could be scientific clues."

Her mother nodded. "They were more concerned with magical clues, like handwriting that can be used to track down people through magic."

Cin grinned. "Mom, go tell the girls to get the library ready, and see if you can help them find me a spell for tracking down a person based on handwriting. I've got something we can go off of." She hadn't bothered trying that with the charms since the process of crafting the charm from molten metal was a good way to remove personal energies from the item made, and the person who crafted the charm wasn't necessarily the person who used it. Using the writing samples on the labels, they'd at least prove if the skeletons in the yard were the ones who scribed the labels. If they weren't, then the Stones were in the wind. If they were, the

# Second-Story Hex

Stones were dead. A tingle of excitement went through Cin as her mother vanished and she gathered some of the jars to take home and cast her spells on them.

# 17

After dinner, while Chad retired to his laptop on the bed, Cin, the girls, and her mother retreated to the library. She made sure to invite her mother in, so she could clear the room's shields without a problem.

"Cool, so we're going to do more magic." EEEK had been bouncing ever since Cin and Chad had picked them up for a quick meal before getting back to work.

"Yes." Cin closed the library door, more out of habit than fear that Chad would interrupt them. She glanced around the room. Everything was cleaned, and there were a couple of books stacked on the desk. "Looks like you girls did a good job cleaning. Now let's see what you found in the books."

Char put the bag with the herb jars in it on the other side of the desk. "Why are there so many jars in here?"

"Just six—" Cin picked up the first book and turned to the page marked with a red piece of paper "—turns out at least four people had a hand in writing on those jars. So we're going to have to do the spell several times."

"Then we probably want to do the simpler spell." Char walked behind her mother and pulled out the book on the bottom of the stack. "I'd do this one."

Cin smiled at her eldest. "Thanks, Char. You're starting to think responsibly. Do we have everything we need for this one?"

After a second of thought, Char nodded. "I'm fairly sure. Nothing in it looked unusual."

"Let me look and I'll get everything." EEEK stared

over Cin's other shoulder as she looked over the spell.

It was a very simple spell that relied more on the caster's own energies than outside herbs or crystals. They could easily link it to the handwriting samples and locate the person who wrote the labels.

"It does my heart good to see you girls so excited about magic." Her mother hovered back by the door looking proud.

"What's not to get excited about?" EEEK walked over to the shelf and pulled out an atlas. "I think this is what we need."

Cin nodded. "That's the important part. We need a pendulum."

"Got it." Char pulled a simple quartz crystal on a cotton string out of her pocket. "Found it earlier."

EEEK stuck her tongue out. "You grabbed it so I couldn't find it."

"Maybe." Char handed the crystal to Cin.

"We also need the local maps." Cin pointed to a drawer in a chest of drawers near the bookshelves.

"I've got it." EEEK raced over. "Do you want the county roads, or the city?"

"Bring both, just in case we need them." Cin set the books they weren't going to be using on the nearest shelf that had space and reached for the county map EEEK brought back.

Unfolded, the map took up most of the desktop. She turned it so it was properly oriented with the south side toward her.

"I made sure to get bottles we could use with the pendulum." Cin reached into the bag and took the bottles out. She arranged them across the top of the desk, lining up the ones that matched, hoping to make the energy flow easier.

"We can do some of them, right?" Char asked.

"Sure. We're working as a team on this." If they

bumped up against the witch Kama had, she hoped by having the four of them working together, it might give her pause in any thought of attacking them. "EEEK, we need a yellow candle."

"Big or little?" EEEK stepped over to the shelf and paused with her hand reaching toward the stacked candles.

"Little will be fine." Cin didn't expect their search to take all night and require a larger candle.

EEEK returned to the desk with a small yellow candle and the square metal candleholder. "Here you go."

"Thank you." Cin smiled as she took the two items and put them on the desk in the center of the top map edge.

"Char, if you could light the candle. EEEK, drop the lights to about twenty five percent." If she'd been working by herself, she'd have used the lights on full, but the girls still needed a bit of ambience to better access their magic, and she was determined to use their search as a learning opportunity.

With a deep breath, Char's energy flashed across the desk and the fresh candlewick burst into flames.

"You're getting good at that, Charlotte." Cin's mother did sound proud of her granddaughter.

"Grandma, when are you going to call me Char like everyone else?" Char had chosen the nickname years early, which had promoted EEEK to go with a nickname as well. Cin's mother hadn't liked it when she was among the living, and that had carried over into her afterlife.

"When you get tired of sounding like a burnt piece of wood and want to be a grownup, Charlotte." The note of disapproval was louder than the note of pride had been moments before.

"Now, now, we have magic to do." Cin drew their attention back to the task at hand. "EEEK, let's get the pendulum tied to the first bottle."

"Okay, Mom." EEEK grabbed the bottle on the far left, then picked up the pendulum on its red cord. She got it tied off quickly, then looked at it. "How are we going to hold it?"

"It's a bit more awkward than the normal pendulum on a chain that most people use, but we need the jar." Cin flattened EEEK's right hand out, surprised at how close to the same size their hands were. Her youngest daughter was easily going to outgrow both her and Chad. She threaded the cord between her middle finger and ring finger. "We're using your right hand because?"

"Because we're going to be projecting power through it… me, to the crystal and the map." EEEK beamed.

"Right." Cin glanced at Char. "You've got the book, let's try this."

There was just enough light for Cin to make out the words of the spell. They had the simple physical parts and they needed to draw power and say the words. She put her hand on EEEK's shoulder, and took Char's hand as Char held the book over the map, between them. Since Cin's mother was incorporeal, she stood in the edge of the desk, completing the circle of the four of them.

Cin didn't bother putting up a proper circle; their power needed to get out into the room, and she'd done enough magic in the library over the years that her defenses there were strong, probably stronger than the ones Kama kept around the shop.

"All right, everybody got the words?" Cin asked as she drew up power and fed it through EEEK, feeling the pendulum swinging randomly from her daughter's hand.

"I want to keep the book open," Char said. "If that's okay."

"It's fine." Cin took in the power Char and her mother were already pushing toward her, and kept it flowing toward EEEK.

"Then I'm ready." Char nodded once.

"Me too." EEEK was trembling with excitement.

Cin knew her mother was ready, and didn't wait for her

response. "Okay, let's do this."

With a uniform breath, they began, four voices raised in simple unison. The spell circled between them, then on the third repetition, it moved out EEEK's hand and down into the pendulum.

The crystal trembled with their power. It swung around in a large, ever-growing arc before it spun down and pointed toward a spot out in the county map. Cin bent over the map and noted the coordinates on a piece of paper. "That was almost too easy."

"We've got three more samples to use." Her mother drew her attention back to the bottles across the top of the map. "And we still don't know who wrote the label, just where they are."

"And that they wrote two of the labels." Cin pointed to the jar behind the empty spot. They still had to determine where exactly that spot in the county was, and who lived there.

"Okay, can I do the next one?" Char asked.

"Sure." Cin watched EEEK untie the first jar and hand the pendulum to her sister.

"We're switching out, right?" EEEK said, then looked at the ghost of her grandmother. "But Grandma won't be able to hold the string, will you, Grandma?"

"No, she won't sweetie, but then we're just going to switch out between you and Char." Cin explained as she took the next jar of herbs and handed it to Char.

"Oh. Cool." EEEK grinned. "It felt really cool when the crystal started to swing."

"Yes, it does." Although Cin had already taught her daughters to use a pendulum, it was different when it was something important like a murder investigation. She totally understood her daughter's excitement. They were getting real-world uses for their magic.

Once Char was ready, they repeated the words from the book. The crystal spun like it had for EEEK, but never spun down to point to anything.

"We need a wider search zone," Cin's mother advised.

"Here." EEEK put the atlas on top of the map. "Where do you want me to open it to?"

"Let's start with the states." Cin took over and opened the book, flipping through until she had the continental US showing. "Okay. Once we can narrow it down to a state, we can try and narrow it down to a town."

"Okay." Char held up the pendulum and they repeated the spell. Again the crystal spun around in a huge arc. It never slowed down to point to a state.

Cin frowned. She'd really hoped that whoever they were after was still in the state, or maybe somewhere close by. If they were on a different continent, that might end up stopping their search hard and fast. They didn't have anything to worry about from a killer in another country.

Over the map of South America they had the same results.

"Hey, maybe they're in Australia," EEEK suggested. "We could spend the summer there chasing them and getting to pet Koalas."

"Nope." Cin shook her head. "If the person is in Australia, they're home free, unless we can get Sheriff Jackson to issue a warrant and let the Australian authorities know that we magically tracked them down to there." She turned the atlas to the southern continent.

"And since we're not supposed to let people know what we can do, that's a resounding no." Chad frowned at her sister, but kept her hand out over the atlas.

"That's right." Cin said. "Now let's do this again."

By the time they made it through all the continents, they still didn't have a lock on the label's writer. Cin changed out bottles to the second one that was in the same hand. Unfortunately, they had the same results. She shook her head. "This doesn't make any sense."

"Unless the writer is now devoid of life." Cin's mother said softly.

Cin stared at her and a chill went through her. "The bones didn't have any useable DNA, or at least that's what Sheriff Jackson told Chad. And DNA is the building blocks of life. How do you wipe the DNA off of bones and still have them hold their shape?"

"Magic, my dear," her mother whispered. "Magic."

By the time they finished with the four different scripts, only two of them had locations, and one of them wouldn't allow them to zoom in any tighter than Cottonwood city limits. When they tried to get a more pinpoint location, the string broke.

"Okay, girls, time for bed. Go get your showers and then kiss your father good night before turning in." Cin pointed up, indicating for them to go upstairs.

Char rolled her eyes. "Mom, when are we going to be too old to kiss Dad goodnight? I had a boyfriend last summer and I didn't kiss him goodnight like I have to do Dad."

"And if you had, your father would've probably eaten him." Cin grinned at the idea of a huge black wolf chasing the skinny kid from camp through the trees around Pagosa Springs.

"Dad wouldn't eat her boyfriends would he?" EEEK asked, wide eyed.

Cin spread her hands and shrugged. "I don't know, that's something to take up with your father."

"If he did, I wouldn't speak to him again," Chad put her hands on her hips. "Are you guys going to be as hard on EEEK when she gets a girlfriend?"

"Probably." Cin nodded her head. "Maybe harder."

"Maaahhhm." EEEK pouted.

"You two go on." She shooed them toward the door. "And thank you for your help tonight. You did great."

# Second-Story Hex

They both stopped and kissed Cin on the cheek before disappearing out the door. A soft quiet of fading footfalls filled the library before she heard them shouting for Chad.

After a moment of stillness, Cin looked at the county map, and then at her notes of the only set of coordinates they'd been able to get. She tapped the map where they were. It was a cow pasture. They drove past it when they headed north out of town. It was one of the few agricultural spots that hadn't become a hemp field. She didn't recall there being a house, shed, or even a tent out that way.

There was something missing, something big, but she couldn't put her finger on what it was.

"Cin are you still down here?" Chad's word preceded his footsteps down the stairs.

"I'm leaving." Cin's mother took a tired breath and looked a little more translucent than normal. The magical workings had taken a bit out of her. Being a creature of energy, expending it normally did. "If you need me, don't hesitate to call."

Cin smiled at her. "Thanks for the help."

"Our girls are coming along wonderfully." Then her mother faded from view.

"You didn't answer me." Chad appeared in the doorway. "But I heard you talking to your mother."

"Just saying goodnight. What's up?" Cin turned from the map to look at her husband. Although he was in a lose T-shirt and sweats, he still looked as put-together as he always did. She wished she could always look nearly perfect the way he did.

"Did you tell Char I was going to eat her next boyfriend?"

Cin laughed. After doing magic, laughing helped finish grounding the energy swirling around her. "Not exactly. I told her if she'd kissed her boyfriend last summer goodnight, you'd probably eat him."

Chad pursed his lips and nodded thoughtfully. "Okay, yeah, I probably would've. These girls thought having a cop for a dad was tough. I really have to fight my over-protective urges a lot more now."

"I know, but you're doing a good job of it." She turned her chair around so he could come in close and give her a hug.

"It's a daily battle sometimes, but I've got you and the girls to help keep me grounded." His arms were strong around her.

"Good."

"So, did you ladies get anything figured out tonight?" He let go of her and leaned on the desk.

"Sort of. Two of the samples were complete busts." Cin turned back to the map. "I think one of them might be our killer, but she's blocking people searching for her. We know she's in town, and that's it. The other one is coming from here." She tapped the spot where the pendulum said the person was.

Chad leaned over and frowned at the map. "There? Are you sure? That's one of the last cow pastures in this part of the county."

Cin nodded. "That's what I thought too."

"We're going to have to go talk to the rancher out there and get permission to sniff around for a body."

"That's what I was afraid you were going to say." She didn't want to go out and find another skeleton, particularly not in some stranger's cow pasture. But if there was enough life in it to be able to get a link between it and the handwriting, Sheriff Jackson might be able to get some DNA. That would be a nice step.

"What about you and missing persons?" Cin wanted to know he'd had a little better luck than she had, but even if they had a list of missing people, they would still have to find a way to link them to the skeletons.

"A few kids, but nothing that matches the skeletons we

found, other than the Stones."

"It keeps swinging back around to the Stones." Cin closed her eyes and rubbed her temples. She was going to have to wait for the girls to get their showers before she could go take a bath, but she wanted time to think and sort out their limited clues and lack thereof.

"Yeah. Do you want me to make a couple of calls to get us permission to go out and search that field?"

"Jackson knows you're a werewolf. Call him and tell him you smelled something out that way. He might just think it's a cow or deer, but it's worth a chance."

Chad took over rubbing her temples. His strong fingers felt great on her head.

Cin sighed as he helped her relax. "Sounds like a decent plan." If they did things the right way, she wouldn't have to be out there as they dug up the body. Maybe she and RJ could finish the demo while Chad handled the dirty work.

# 18

"It was right where you said it would be," Chad said as soon as Cin answered his call the next afternoon.

She wiped demo dust off her face. "Good. Any sign of more charms?"

"Sorta." Chad replied. "I'll send you pictures in a couple of minutes, if I can do it without getting caught. It doesn't look complete, like the other ones."

"Complete?" Cin tried to figure out what he was talking about.

"It's not as complex. Look, I gotta go. Call you on the way back to town." He hung up quickly, leaving Cin wonder what was going on.

"You look perplexed." RJ banged his gloved hands together, sending up a puff of dust.

"They found another skeleton where I thought it would be." Cin looked around. The kitchen was down to the studs. "Chad said there was another charm but it wasn't complete."

"Maybe it was an earlier attempt." RJ glanced around. "I think we're done in here, for the moment."

"Yeah, both of those sound about right." Cin started toward the bedroom, where the master bath still had a couple of cabinets to come out. "I wish we had a way to date the bones, to know which came first. Chad said he was going to see about getting me a picture of it if he could do it without getting into trouble."

"Might be helpful." RJ stopped in the door to the bathroom. "Want to help me get these out and then we can send the guys home, unless you've ordered the sheetrock we need to replace."

"Sure. Haven't gotten that ordered yet." Cin glanced around and spotted a pry bar on the floor in front of the cabinet. "We also still have to work on the basement."

"I can't seem to get that one door open, might just use the saws-all on it and be done with it."

"Good idea. I'll help when we get this out."

She picked up the pry bar as a woman's voice called out. "Hello?"

Cin turned toward the front room. "We're back here!" She tried to place the voice, but couldn't.

Moments later, Lucille Jackson walked in. "Cinnamon Kilkari, I'd heard you were working on this house and had to come and see what you've done with the place." She stopped over the magical symbol that had been covered up with black paint after one of the demo crew had said it made him nervous. Her shiny cowgirl boots with their metal toes were just on the edge of where the circle had been.

As she stared at the sheriff's wife, Cin repressed a shiver. The couple of other times she'd met the statuesque woman she'd been a little intimidated, but the look on her face was one of judgement, not so much intimidation. She seemed to be weighing something about Cin in her hard gaze.

"Hello, Mrs. Jackson. Nice of you to stop by." Cin set the pry bar down on the edge of the cabinet, making sure it wouldn't crash to the floor. She pulled off her gloves and strode to the other woman, noting the odd way the light coming through the skylight struck her deep auburn hair and turned it to an almost blood red. Holding out her hand, she wasn't sure if she wanted Lucille Jackson to touch her or not.

"Well, I was a little surprised to hear that Solstice Properties were turning their eyes on the county beyond the city limits and it piqued my interest." Her hand was almost winter cold as it closed around Cin's fingers. Luckily their contact was fairly short.

"You can blame that on Marzie Campbell; she thought we might be interested in it." Cin stopped herself from wiping her hand on her dusty jeans as Lucille let go of her.

An unreadable look marred Lucille's face for a moment, then it was gone. "Marzie Campbell. I understand that her business is growing. With the legal grows popping up, I bet a lot of people are looking for places out here."

"That's my understanding."

Lucille glanced at the floor where the dark paint obscured the magical symbol that had been part of the trap spell. "You've done a lot with the place so far. Maybe you'll let me come see it when you get done. I didn't know the Stones well, but they were neighbors for years."

Cin nodded slowly. "That's what Shelby said, that you'd lived next door for a while."

"Yes. Honestly, I think we probably would move to Denver if Nick didn't love his job so much. When he retires, we'll be there before his replacement gets his badge tarnished." She looked around, but her gaze didn't linger on one thing too long. "I have to admit that I'm about done with the dirt and dust that comes from living around here. It was quaint enough when Nick was starting his career, but I never dreamed we'd end up stuck out here. Even living in Cottonwood doesn't seem to be enough for me anymore."

"Cottonwood isn't for everyone." Cin wished the woman would just move on so they could get back to work.

"This might sound like an odd question, but Nick mentioned that you'd found some skeletons in the back yard." She paused and looked out the window that oversaw the yard. "What other strange things have you encountered?"

Cin shrugged. "Since the Stones disappeared without a trace and when we got in, it didn't look like anyone but Marzie had been in here in years. There really wasn't anything odd, so to speak, just the regular things that people leave behind when they vanish. Since all their clothes, dishes, and toiletries were still here, I really think the bodies we found are them. But from what Shelby said, you and Sheriff Jackson were living next door at the time. I would figure if something bad took place here, you'd know about it."

Lucille instantly shook her head and raised a hand if to ward off the question. "I came over a couple of times, but didn't really know the Stones. Luckily the hedge between the properties was high enough to block their lights at night. I never even knew if they were coming or going."

Not wanting to argue, since the hedge wasn't an evergreen and odds were, it didn't block much during the winter months, Cin let the comment go. It sounded like something Lucille had come up with to cover her for something.

The lights flickered and died.

RJ frowned. "That's odd. If you ladies will excuse me, I'm going to go check the breaker box."

"Of course." Cin waved him out.

"These old houses do have questionable wiring at times." Lucille stepped toward the window, but managed to ease into the shadow next to it.

Cin looked at the woman. It almost felt like she'd done something, but Cin hadn't felt anything in the way of magic coming off her.

One of the demo crew rushed in. "Miss Cin, the transformer, it is on fire." He pointed out front of the house.

"Crap." Cin ran toward the front of the house, totally forgetting Lucille Jackson. If the transformer was on fire, they could be in for a big problem; they didn't need the house to burn down before they could figure out what to do with it.

RJ came in from the kitchen. "What's wrong? Breakers look fine."

Cin pointed out the front door. "Transformer."

"I'm calling 911." RJ stopped just outside the front door staring up as Cin went past him into the yard.

Sparks and flames fountained out of the transformer on the pole across the dirt road from the house. The wires running from the pole came directly to them.

"Get the cars and trucks out of the way." Cin pointed toward the vehicles that were under the wires. She hoped they could get things moved before the wires came crashing down.

"I guess I'd better go." Lucille appeared beside Cin. "The fire department should be here quickly. The volunteer station is just down the street." She gestured to the left. "Please call me when you get everything done. I'd love to see the house brought back to some semblance of glory."

Cin started down the steps toward her car. "I will. Thanks for stopping by."

Lucille hurried across the yard to a sleek sedan parked on the road, well away from the burning wires.

The demo crew was already in their truck and driving away. Cin hadn't meant for them to leave for the day, then realized the fewer people under foot when the fire department got there, the better.

She got in her car and started it as RJ dashed past to his truck. They both got the vehicles moved out into the street and far enough away to not cause problems for the volunteer fire department when they arrived.

As Cin got out of her car, the wire running from the transformer to their pole gave way and fell into the roll-away dumpster. The dried wood instantly sparked and caught fire.

"Hoses!" RJ shouted and ran toward the house.

Cin followed, thankful she was in work shoes that would handle running.

In the distance, sirens rang out.

Grabbing the end of the garden hose, Cin hoped the thing would handle the pressure of water going through it. It felt dry and ready to fall apart.

After a bit of straining, RJ got the faucet to turn and the hose tightened in Cin's hands before water erupted from the end. She ran around the corner of the house and got as close as she dared, holding her thumb over the end of the hose to cause the water to spray farther. She wished there was a nozzle on it, but it was enough to reach the dumpster that had erupted into a mass of flames and smoke.

"Cin, be careful, no telling what's been in those walls."

She nodded and was thankful the wind was blowing the smoke away from them. Wind. It was howling around them. She hadn't noticed it earlier in the day, or even when they had run for the cars, but the wind was blowing hard and pushing the flames toward the house.

The first fire truck pulled up and several burly men piled out and started unrolling hoses.

One man ran over to her. "Ma'am, are you the owner?"

"Yes." Cin glanced at him for a moment, but wanted to keep her focus on the fire. If she'd stopped to think about it, she would've tried to craft a shield or ward to protect the house, but she'd always been taught, and had taught her daughters to find a mundane solution first and resort to magic as a last resort. She kept the water going. With the firemen there, she wasn't about to try anything out of the ordinary to stop the flames.

"We can handle things from here." The fireman reached for the hose.

"Thanks." Cin relinquished the hose to the professional.

"We've got a call to the power company to get out here and take care of that transformer." He nodded toward the still-sparking and flaming hunk of metal. The flames were starting down the power-pole toward the greening grass where unfortunately there was also a large amount of dried grass and weeds that would take off quickly.

"Come on, Cin." RJ touched her arm, and nodded

toward their cars by the road. "Let's get out of their way."

Getting over to the cars would give her the opportunity to do a bit of protective magic without being seen by the firemen. She followed him across the yard as a second fire truck, a big tanker, pulled up, perfectly timed to match when the firemen unrolling the hoses were getting everything ready to do their thing and put out the dumpster fire. The way the men were all over the yard, she was thankful they hadn't gotten to putting in the new sod that would make the place look so much better.

They got to their vehicles. RJ leaned against his truck. "These guys are good, for volunteers."

"They have to be, or they'd lose a lot more houses than they do." Cin pulled out her phone and dialed Chad. "You won't believe who stopped by." She didn't even wait for him to finish saying hello.

"Who?"

"Lucille Jackson." Cin sighed and leaned against her car as the first spray of water arched out of the firehose and hit the dumpster.

"What? Why?"

"Well, we can get to that in a second. When she left, we had a dumpster fire to deal with."

"Wait. What?"

She took a moment and explained about the fire.

"Stay out of the way, I'll be there as fast as I can." In the background his car door slammed and his engine roared to life.

"Don't worry about it. The firemen have it under control, and the power company just got here. They should have the transformer down in a few minutes." She turned her attention from the firemen to the power company truck that was down at the pole closer to town than the one on fire. They had a basket going up.

"I think I'll head home then. Be careful and keep me in the loop."

"I will. I love you."

"Love you too." Chad hung up.

Cin looked from the house to the linemen who were cutting the cables at the other pole. "Guess we're not going to have power for a couple of days."

RJ shrugged. "Depending on how quickly they get the pole fire put out, maybe just a couple of hours. I can come out tomorrow morning, check and let you know."

"That would be good. Or I could send Chad out first thing, he could probably be back before I'm even ready to get out of bed. He's a major early bird." Cin breathed a slight sigh of relief as the flames in the dumpster died back and only a little smoke curled out of it. They weren't going to lose the house; that was good.

"You two discuss it and let me know. I'm flexible." RJ huffed and watched the firemen. "I was really hoping on finishing the demo today."

Cin pursed her lips. "I think we came real close to finishing it and not in the way we'd planned."

"There is that." RJ crossed his arms and nodded. "A little too freaky if you ask me."

"I agree." Cin looked down the road, toward the direction Lucille Jackson had driven off, not back to Cottonwood, but toward Monte Vista. She might've been trying to avoid the traffic of the firetrucks she would've known were coming, but there could be another reason. Maybe she had to visit friends or family, or just wanted a pleasant drive in the country, although that didn't seem to in her character, based on what she'd said about being tired of the area.

The fire was bothersome, in more ways than most people would think. Sure, it could've been coincidence, but Cin wasn't a big fan of coincidence, particularly when dealing with a place that had already had magical happenings about. Fire and electricity were both basic elements, things magic users could control. If they were stirring a bigger hornet's nest than they thought, someone might be trying to cover their tracks.

# 19

When Cin walked into the house, Chad wrapped her in his strong arms and gave her a big hug and a kiss. "I'm so glad you're okay. What happened?"

"Officially, or what I think happened?" Reluctantly Cin stepped out of his arms and headed for the kitchen. She needed a bottle of water. She and RJ had stayed at the house until the fire fighters had the dumpster and the area around the base of the pole put out, and the power company had the wires cut and requested a new transformer. The linemen didn't seem too worried, saying a lot of the transformers in the area were old and in need of replacement. It seemed they blew on a regular basis. The biggest concern was fire.

"I think officially it was a transformer blowing out." Chad followed her into the kitchen and hopped up on the counter, then glanced around. "I didn't just sit in your mother, did I?"

Cin shook her head. "I haven't seen Mom today. I know the seeking spells last night wore her out. Might be a day or so before she tries to materialize again."

"Oh." Chad nodded. "So, you don't think it was just a transformer blowing out?"

"I don't know for sure." Cin opened the water bottle and took a long drink. "I find the whole things kinda suspicious. Lucille Jackson shows up to see what we're doing with the house, and the transformer blows."

"Did you feel any magic from her?"

"No." Cin set the water on the counter near Chad. "But she also knew where the trap spell was. And the really strange thing, she seemed a little pissed that Marzie showed us the house."

"Pissed?" Chad wrinkled his brow. "I can't say as I've ever seen Lucille Jackson as anything beyond controlled and maybe a bit icy."

"There's that too, but that icy exterior got a little hot under the collar, for just a couple of seconds when I mentioned Marzie showing us the house. It could be just my imagination." Cin picked up the water and took another drink. "I almost wish Mom had been out there with us. As a ghost, she's a little more sensitive to things like that than I am."

"So you've been saying. Yeah, I would like to hear what Charity has to say about that and about this latest body having an incomplete charm." Chad pulled out his phone and opened a picture for Cin to look at. "What do you think?"

Before she looked too long, Cin pulled out her own phone and glanced at the pictures of the first charms. The basic layout with the familiar runes were nearly the same. She took Chad's phone from him and laid both phones on the counter so she could better study them. "This is interesting. It's the symbols I haven't been able to locate that are missing from the new one, or should we say the old one."

"You're probably right, the one we found today was a first try, or an earlier try." Chad looked over Cin's shoulder.

"Who would know what these marks mean?" Cin wished they had a larger magical community in Cottonwood. Someone might have access to knowledge she didn't.

"Have you looked online?" Chad hopped off the counter and bent to pop his neck.

Cin shook her head. "Not yet. Might be time to do so though." She let out a long breath. "I don't want to just go out there and start asking questions in forums and such, you never know what kind of crazy crackpot response you're going to get."

"Then don't ask for help, just yet." Chad wrapped his

arms around her waist. "Just look for pictures."

"And how do we do that? Do a search for death runes, or anti-life charms?"

"How about we isolate the symbols you don't know, and then do an image match?"

"A what?" Cin turned and stared at him. He was always more up-to-date on technology than she was, and sometimes that got to be irritating.

"An image match." He walked over to the tool drawer and pulled out a small pad of paper and a pen. "Here. Draw one of the ones you're having trouble finding."

Cin drew out one of the symbols. She didn't like the strange feeling it left in her hand as she did. Just drawing it seemed to attract shadows to her. With a shiver, she put the pen down.

"Okay. Let's take a picture of that." Chad held his phone over the pad and snapped an image. He glanced at the phone, then pulled up a program. "Give me a second and we'll know if this symbol is anywhere that's been indexed on the web."

It was Cin's turn to look over his shoulder. She leaned against his back as he watched the turning hourglass on his phone. If there was one thing she hated, it was waiting for programs to do their thing. In a world of instant gratification, not having immediate results irritated her.

Less than a minute later, an image popped up, and then a couple of more.

"Mayan death symbol?" Chad looked from the screen to Cin.

"Or someone's interpretation of it." Cin frowned at the chunky image that was only vaguely similar to what she had drawn. There were major risks when changing powerful symbols. She didn't know anyone local who dealt with Mayan magics. Kama might know of someone who did, or they might have to go to Albuquerque to find a practitioner.

She took the phone from him and pulled up the page the image was from. It was an archeological page that said they weren't entirely sure what the symbol was used for. It was seen in most of the pyramids across Central America.

Cin made a couple of notes about Mayan magic and put a question mark about death symbol before she went back and pulled up some of the other pages. The other pages gave her more of the same, and none of them were from practitioners who might know the magical uses of the symbol.

"Okay. Let's try one of the others." Cin pulled up the charm photos and jotted down one of the other symbols.

Before they could get a shot of it with Chad's phone, Cin's phone rang. It was Marzie.

"Cin?" She sounded horrible.

"Marzie, what's wrong?" Cin put the phone on speaker so Chad could listen in.

"My office. It just burned down."

Cin stared at Chad. She didn't believe in coincidence, and having Marzie's office burn down right after Lucille Jackson had most likely caused a fire at the Stone house was too much to write off. "Are you okay?"

"Yeah." Her breath came heavily. "At least physically. They said a transformer blew and set the roof on fire."

A chill went through Cin. "A transformer blew?"

Too much of a coincidence. She wanted to know more about Lucille Jackson, and quickly, before someone else's place burned down, or worse, their own.

Cin looked up from her magical books as Char and EEEK came down the stairs.

"You're home early." Char stopped in the doorway. "Dad said something about a fire."

"Two fires actually. So we're going to do a few things to protect us from a fire." Cin spun the book around and handed it to Char. "We've already got last-year's mistletoe hanging over the front door, we're going to go a little beyond that."

EEEK frowned. "Do you think we're under attack? Why would anyone do that?"

"I think it's tied to the skeletons your father found, and he did find another one where you said it would be." Cin patted EEEK on the hand.

Her youngest beamed. "Rad."

Char finished looking over the protection spell. "This one's fairly straightforward. We should be able to get it done before dinner."

Cin chuckled. "Definitely. Let's get it done so you girls can do your homework."

"Mom." EEEK rolled her eyes. "Magic is so much more important than homework."

"They are both important," Cin countered. "But today, magic first, then homework."

"Okay." EEEK bounced a bit.

"Char, get me the mistletoe, the dragon's blood, and the sage. EEEK, run up and get me the big thing of salt." Cin instructed the girls, then got and retrieved a white candle from the shelf.

Moments later, EEEK returned with the bucket of salt. "Do you need all of it?"

Cin shook her head. "No, but run back up and grab a gallon Ziplock bag for me. We're going to need it to do some mixing."

"Okay." EEEK set the container of salt on the floor next to the desk and disappeared back up the stairs.

"We're a little short on the dragon's blood." Char held up the bottle of rusty resin.

"It'll have to do." Cin looked at the book. The spell called for equal parts of dragon's blood and mistletoe.

Char pointed to the jars Cin had brought from the

house. "There's some dragon's blood in there."

"No." Cin shook her head. "Never use someone else's components if you can at all help it. We don't know where they've been."

"Oh." Char put the jars from their cupboard on the desk.

"Okay, I got the bag." EEEK dashed into the room waving the clear plastic bag around.

"Good. Now, the salt is just the carrier for everything else." Cin opened up the Ziplock and held it for EEEK to start filling. "Let's fill the bag about half way."

Char stared at them. "Why so much?"

"It's going all the way around the property. We're going to protect the chickens and everything." Cin made a large circle with her finger.

"Oh." Char nodded. "I thought it was just going around the house."

Cin shook her head. "Not good enough. We don't want anything to happen to anything that might be in the yard if an attack comes."

"Yeah, the chickens deserve to live too." EEEK stopped adding salt to the bag and put her hands on her hips and glared at her sister.

"I agree." Char held up her hands in surrender.

"Good." Cin set the bag of salt on the desk. "Always remember that we need to protect everyone, and everything that relies on us. It's one of the things that separates us from black witches."

"Do you think that's what we're dealing with?" Char dumped all the mistletoe they had into the bag of salt.

"Maybe. At this point, I'm not really sure." Cin didn't want to scare her daughters more than she needed to. They were dealing with magic she wasn't used to, and that wasn't a good thing. The fact that the first symbol they'd looked up had been Mayan told her that whoever was crafting the charms knew more than she did, in the realm of magic, knowledge was power. The other symbols were other kinds of magic she'd never dealt with, the Thuggee one scared her almost as badly as the Mayan.

They got all the ingredients into the bag and took turns shaking it all together while they drew up power and chanted the words of the spell. After the salt was glowing with their power, Cin declared it ready. She sent the girls up to encircle the yard with their salt mixture while she stayed at the desk, making sure their shield went up easily. Sure, the salt might leave scorch marks on their grass, but that was a lot better than their house getting burned down by another malfunctioning transformer.

When they were done, she breathed a little easier, and while the girls settled into their homework, she told Chad and headed to Marzie's house, hoping to get some answers as to what was going on. If Lucille, or whoever was behind the skeletons, had taken anger out on Marzie, she had to know more than she'd told them about the Stones, and the house in general.

**20**

Marzie looked horrible when she answered the door. Cin stepped in and gave her a big hug.

"Would you like some whiskey?" Marzie asked as she stepped out of Cin's hug. "It's been a whiskey sort of day."

Cin shook her head, trying to remember if she'd ever seen Marzie so wide-eyed and shaken. "No thanks. Come, sit and tell me what happened."

With a heavy sigh, Marzie walked deeper into the house. She went straight to the couch and poured herself another glass of Old Crow from the half-empty bottle on the coffee table.

Plopping down on the floral pattern couch, Marzie downed a quarter of the glass and thunked it back on the thick glass tabletop. "Where to start...oh...it's all gone. My whole office went up in flames. All my files are gone, just ash." She burst into tears.

Cin sat next to her and put an arm across her shoulders. "But you got out alive, that's the most important thing. You can rebuild."

Marzie sniffled. "Why? What's the point of trying to rebuild?"

"People always rebuild after accidents, right?" Cin wasn't sure what to say. The woman next to her wasn't close to the person she remembered as her friend. Marzie was always upbeat and perky, ready to try and gloss over any little imperfection in a home she was showing, or try to turn a flaw into a benefit. The woman on the couch was lost, adrift in a way Marzie hadn't been in years.

"But I've got too much to rebuild from. Jerry, the grabber, now this." She took another drink of her whiskey. "I think I'm being told to at least get out of Cottonwood, maybe out of real estate. But this is my home, it has been for years. I've been happy here. I don't want to leave."

Cin squeezed Marzie's shoulders a little tighter. "And we don't want you to leave."

"Thanks." Marzie patted Cin's hand on her shoulder. "I think you and Chad are the last friends I've got around here. So much going on, it's like the whole area has turned on me."

She sighed, laid her head against Cin's shoulder and started crying again.

Cin sat there and held her, thankful she'd thought to come over. Marzie needed someone, badly.

As her crying slowed down, Cin relaxed a little. "Marzie, where's Little Jerry?" Although her son wasn't so little anymore, everyone still called him Little Jerry since he wasn't as big as his father yet.

"I thought it might be safer for him to go stay with friends for the night. You know teenagers, always up for getting away from their parents." Marzie sniffled hard. "After this, he might just want to move to Denver with his father and his floozy. He might be safer. They were willing to take out my office, they might be willing to burn down the house too."

Having just wrapped her own house in protective anti-fire magic, Cin straightened a little. "Why do you think someone burned you down?"

Marzie gave a weak laugh. "They said it was a transformer, but that's really convenient isn't it? What's the odds of three transformers blowing in this town on the same day, particularly if the winds weren't up at the time?"

"Three?" Cin stared at her friend, she was only aware of two.

"Yeah, the one above Third Eye Open also blew, but there was no damage from that one. All the sparks died before they hit the ground. But the police closed off the area just to be safe while the power company replaced the transformer. You didn't hear about that. I figured they still had Chad in the loop for everything." Marzie finished off her whiskey and set the glass down, staring at the bottle as if trying to decide if she wanted more or not.

"We missed that one, but it's been a busy day." Cin wanted to go check on Kama, but if the shop was still in one piece, that was good. Kama's protections were strong and it would take a coven working major magic to do any damage to her. A call when she left Marzie would suffice.

"I think we should've left well enough alone, Cin. The Stone house isn't worth all this. The place should just be burned down and let all the ghosts be scattered to the wind with the smoke." Marzie leaned back against the couch without filling another glass of whiskey.

"Marzie, do you know more about what happened out there? Do you know who's doing this?" Cin didn't think her friend had ever even played with magic. Her thresholds at home and the office were no stronger than normal. There weren't any unusual statuary or books about. But then most people who entered Cin's home and office wouldn't spot anything, unless they noticed the protections around the places.

Marzie shrugged. "I don't know. Not for sure. Just rumors."

Cin thought that since Chad was an ex-cop they were fairly high on the rumor ladder, but maybe she was wrong. Marzie was out seeing people's houses, selling places and sometimes getting into homes of recluses who were unknown even to their neighbors. "Rumors can be a good place to start."

"Yeah." A weak chuckle escaped Marzie. "I think there are witches in town. I don't just mean Kama over at Third

Eye, or that gal over at Open Mind bookstore. Cin, I've seen some crazy stuff, and I don't think we were supposed to find those skeletons. Even if they aren't the Stones, someone was killed out there and now somebody else wants to cover it up and is willing to use magic to do so."

"It looks like that, doesn't it?" Cin shivered slightly.

"How else do you explain them burning my office down?" Marzie sighed and shook her head. "Jerry had been telling me for years to start backing up to the cloud, or whatever. He'd say don't keep everything there in the office. Offsite storage. But I didn't understand all of it. So much is so confusing. And now my office is gone. Burned to the ground. It's just ashes."

Before Cin could respond, the doorbell rang. "Do you want me to get that?"

"I'm not up for people right now." Marzie reached past Cin for the whiskey bottle.

"Okay." Cin stood and hurried to the door.

Shelby, their yoga instructor, stood there when she opened the door. She was one of the people in town closer to Marzie than Cin was. "Oh, god, Cin. Is she alright?"

"Not good." Cin said, prepared to try and block Shelby, but she slipped under Cin's arm and down the entryway.

"Marzie. Oh my god. This is terrible."

"Shelby. Thank you for caring enough to come. I really think I'm cursed," Marzie said after the clink of the whiskey bottle hitting the coffee table rang out.

Cin closed the door and headed back to the living room. She had hoped that Marzie had been about to spill the beans on who she thought might be doing magic against her, and others involved with the skeletons, but with Shelby there, they were going to have to go through everything again. There were good odds that by the time they were done, Marzie would be too drunk to be remotely coherent.

Shelby had taken Cin's spot on the couch, but since

Marzie was in the middle of the sofa, Cin took her other side. Marzie was already in the retelling, it was going to be a long night, and Cin hoped whoever was working against them had worn themselves out blowing three transformers in a day. That kind of magic wasn't easy. But then if they were being eclectic and drawing power from various sources, any deities willing to cause chaos for them, they were more dangerous than any witch or wizard Cin had encountered before.

She was beginning to think that maybe someone had cursed Marzie, but they had other problems as well. It was going to take more digging to get to the core of the bigger problems.

# 21

Cin stared at the outside of the jewelry store that was part classy boutique and part tourist trap. On the eastern edge of Cottonwood, it was the last place on her list of shops to check. Cottonwood was so small it didn't have the call for more than a few jewelry stores, and Cin had already been to the other two that morning, with no luck in finding anyone doing lost wax casting. The other shops had been only sales outlets and hadn't done any custom work. They'd bith pointed her to Silver Mountain.

"You used to wear a lot of silver." Her mother appeared in the passenger seat. "It is the most magical of the metals."

"And is guaranteed to burn Chad if I were to touch him with it." Cin reached through her mother for her purse. The sunlight coming through the window glistened off the diamond in her wedding band, which was white gold. Overall, she didn't mind not wearing silver, although she had several ceremonial pieces that she occasionally missed wearing.

As she opened the door, she paused. The charms hadn't been silver, they'd been brass or bronze. Had that been because the person crafting had been a lycanthrope of some sort, or was it because the other metals were cheaper? She wasn't positive if brass or bronze would be crafted the same, but thought she'd seen a fair amount of silver, gold or platinum. It was something to ask around about and find out.

Her mother drifted after her. "You know, Chad has never been one to participate in your magic. You could go back to using silver jewelry there. The two of you are going to make it harder on the girls as they start getting their own pieces."

"I'm sure if they decide to wear silver in the future, they'll remember to keep it well away from Chad. We'll talk more when we get back to the car." Cin opened the door to the shop and strolled in. If she'd put her Bluetooth headset in, she could've claimed she was on a call while she talked with her mother, but didn't like diverting her attention, particularly when she was trying to figure out what was going on with the Stone house.

The door she'd chosen opened into the tourist part of the store. There were shelves full of Colorado branded knickknacks and clothing. The boutique was down at the far end of the building.

"You used to love this cheap stuff," her mother commented as they walked along the shelves of snow globes and pet rocks. "You had that rock, what did you call it?"

"Sydney," Cin muttered, hoping nobody was close enough to hear her.

"That's right. Sydney." Her mother chuckled. "You were so convinced that nobody could be allergic to a rock."

"And I was right." Cin stepped down a half step going from the cheaper items to the more expensive. The floor went from worn linoleum to polished tile.

As the sound of her boot heels on the tile cut through the silence, a clerk stood from behind the counter. There hadn't been a chime that Cin had heard, so the clerk must've known to look up at the sound of shoes on the tile, and probably totally ignored the people walking around in the tourist area as long as she could.

"Hi, if I can show you anything, let me know." The middle-aged woman had her long black hair tied back in a braid that draped down her chest.

"Actually, I'm trying to find out if there's anyone around who can do custom, lost wax jewelry." Cin walked straight to her, ignoring everything else in the small shop.

## Second-Story Hex

The clerk pursed her lips and looked thoughtful. "I don't know of anyone around town anymore. Times changed and the craftsmen and women who used to do it have either gone out of business or died."

It was the first spark of hope she'd had. "Gone out of business? So there were some people at one time?"

"Yes." The woman nodded, making her braid bob. "I think Vivian was the last one, and she sold us this shop five years ago."

"I remember Vivian, a really nice lady," Cin's mother said.

The woman turned toward her with a look of confusion on her face. It was almost like she could hear Cin's mother.

"Do you know if Vivian is still in Cottonwood? Or around here?" It was a long shot, but it was the first possible path to resolving the mystery they'd had in a couple of days.

"She is. But she's not doing jewelry anymore. She's just not up for it."

"Any chance that while she was doing it, she taught classes?" Cin knew she was reaching, but the idea that the person they were looking for might have crafted the charms themselves seemed more likely than having them crafted, particularly with the one Chad had found in the field had been more primitive than the ones on the skeletons, and less effective.

The clerk nodded again. "She did. She had hoped of finding an apprentice to carry on her work after she wasn't able to."

"I like that idea." Cin smiled, hoping to put the clerk more at ease. "So many of the skills and crafts are getting lost in the digital rush."

"And the cheap stuff flooding the market." The clerk smiled back.

"That too."

"Vivian used to have several classes she offered, but

**145**

none of her students decided to go into things full force. There were a couple of people who got into precious metal clay work, but it's not the same as lost wax."

It wasn't something Cin had heard of. "Precious metal clay?"

The clerk nodded. "Yes. It's really easy to craft and then you have to burn it. The clay melts away leaving just the metal."

Cin pulled out her phone and pulled up one of the closeups of the more refined charms. "Any chance this was done with metal clay?"

"Madre Dios." The clerk crossed herself. "Do you think someone used Vivian's classes to make that? It's horrible."

"We don't know." Cin kept the phone held out to the woman, even after her reaction. "We think these were used to kill someone."

The clerk nodded, then looked back at the phone. "Very possible. Evil. It is possible it was metal clay. The work is fairly clean, which you get with wax, but there would be a lot of detail work in wax, it would be easier in clay. Hard to say from a picture."

"Would Vivian be able to tell the difference?" Cin turned the phone off and slipped it into her pocket.

"Yes. Vivian is a master craftswoman." The clerk looked a little nervous.

"Where is Vivian? Would it be possible to visit with her on this? I can't get anyone else in town to help out." Cin didn't like sounding desperate, but she was getting that way.

"She's in the assisted living downtown." The woman pursed her lips and sighed. "I can't remember the name of the place. It's very nice."

"I think I know where you're talking about." Cin stood and gave the woman a parting smile. "Thanks for your help."

"Find the person who uses such evil. We do not need them in Cottonwood." She crossed herself again, then spat on the floor.

"Doing my best." Cin hurried away from the counter and toward her car. She hoped she'd be able to locate Vivian at the assisted living and that Vivian might be able to help her figure out who made the charms.

"Do you remember Vivian's last name?" Cin and her mother drove toward the central part of Cottonwood.

Her mother's forehead wrinkled in thought. "Oro. Yes, I'm fairly sure it was Oro."

As they stopped for one of the three lights in town, Cin stared at her. "Oro? The silversmith's name translates to gold?"

"Sure. Why not. Some people like irony."

The light changed and Cin turned her attention back to the road. "Okay. It's just a bit odd."

"And our family isn't odd?"

"Not in the same way." Cin hit the brakes as a coyote dashed out in front of her with a squirrel in its mouth.

"Chaos coming our way," her mother said as she turned her head, following the way the coyote ran.

Cin rolled her eyes. "Like anything could get any more chaotic than it already is."

"Don't tempt gods like that." Her mother shook a finger at her. "They often take that as a challenge."

"If there's one thing we don't need to do right now, it's challenge gods." Cin turned and realized too late that the parking lot for the assisted living was a sharp turn and she had to go down the block and come back to make it into the lot.

Seconds after getting into the lot, she found a place near the front door. As she headed in through the front doors, loud, badly-played music rumbled out into the street. It sounded just slightly better than one of the neighbor's kids had been the previous summer when he and a couple of friends had tried to start a garage band. Whoever was playing the drums was in desperate need of more lessons.

A woman closed a heavy wooden door, cutting off a large amount of the 'music' as she headed toward the reception desk. "Sorry about that. Music therapy has been trying more modern music, since more of the residents grew up wanting to be Elvis or the Beetles, it makes sense to move beyond the old-time hymns they used to use."

She explained so much in her opening lines. Cin couldn't help but grin and wonder what the world of music therapy was going to be like when she and her generation got there and the kinds of music were much wider-ranged. The sudden image of old men wanting to be Ozzy flooded her head, then she realized that Ozzy was an old man and hadn't slowed down in the least.

"No worries. I've heard good things about music therapy." Cin closed the distance with the desk so she didn't have to struggle to be heard over the music.

"It's wonderful, although we have occasionally had fights break out since we're a multigenerational facility, and a lot of times, social skills are the first thing that starts slipping with some of the residents who are here for memory issues." The woman grinned. "We try to be as accommodating to our residents and their families as possible."

"That's great." Cin grinned back. "I understand that an old friend of my mother's is a resident here. Vivian Oro?"

The receptionist's grin broadened. "Ms. Oro. Yes, she's in the art room at her regular table. I swear she spends more time fixing other resident's broken jewelry than she does anything else."

"That sounds like her." Cin tried to make it sound like she knew Vivian, in hopes that the receptionist would point her in the right direction and then let her go.

"If you'd sign in, that'd be great." She pointed to the clipboard in the center of her counter. "I can..." Her phone rang, cutting her off.

She quickly answered it. "Oh…yeah, I'll be right there." She hung up and glanced at the clipboard. "Ms. Kilkari, if you'd please follow me. The art room is on my way to help a resident."

"I don't want to be a problem." Cin did her best to look harmless.

The receptionist shook her head. "No problem. Like I said, it's on the way."

She led Cin down a hallway. All of the doors were decorated with various spring and summer items, some had resident's names, and some were just numbers. At a T in the hall, the receptionist stopped. "Okay, see that door over there next to the glass wall?" She pointed at the next door on the hall.

Cin nodded. "Sure."

"That's the art room. Ms. Oro should be in there."

"Thanks." Cin waved and gave her a huge smile before heading on into the room.

The art room had several large tables with a mishmash of chairs scattered around them. Each table seemed to have a different type of art going on, some simple, almost childish art with cardboard and finger paints, and others where fake flowers were waiting to be twisted into wreaths. A stooped old woman sat at the far table with a small assortment of tools and wire. She looked up and smiled. "You must be Charity's girl."

Cin stopped and stared. "Yes. How do you know that?"

Vivian Oro set her pliers down and smiled. "Your mother's standing right beside you. Hello Charity. How's the afterlife treating you?"

Cin's mother smiled back. "It's so nice being seen by more than family. I always thought you had the sight."

"Comes and goes anymore." Vivian waved off the comment. "Not that my gifts were ever very good."

# A.M. Burns

The fact that Vivian sounded like she was in command of her facilities, Cin decided to cut straight to the chase. If her mother wanted to hang out and spend time with an old friend, that would be her call. "Ms. Oro, I'm hoping you can tell me who made these, or at least what method was used to craft them." She pulled up the pictures on her phone and turned it around so Vivian could see it.

Vivian pursed her lips and frowned in concentration. "I've never seen anything like this, but there have been a couple of people who took my class years ago who might've done it." She wasn't acting as horrified as the woman at the shop had done.

"Do you remember names, or which class they took?"

"I'm not really great with names these days." She tapped the table thoughtfully. "There were three women who took the class together, one of the few times I didn't have ladies just wanting to make silver crosses. Silver crosses are very big in crafting classes here in the valley."

Cin nodded. "I've seen some very pretty ones."

Vivian's grin broadened. "I bet some of them were mine. They sold really well, both to the locals and the tourists."

"I bet they did." Cin was well aware of the predominant Catholic leanings of the local Hispanic population.

"Yes, always lots of crosses."

"Vivian," Cin's mother spoke up. "What about the three women who didn't want to make crosses?"

"They seemed very close." Vivian suddenly sounded far away. "It was so unusual to have the chance to make something other than crosses."

"Why did they seem close?" Cin hoped to find a way to refocus the older woman.

A lopsided grin crept across Vivian's face, like she was suddenly somewhere else. "I made some very nice crosses over the years. I won prizes with my crosses."

Cin wanted to snap her fingers and try to draw her back,

but she wasn't sure what was the proper way to deal with someone like Vivian. When her mother had passed away, it had been a fast heart attack. They hadn't had to deal with any declining mental facilities. If they had, Cin had occasionally wondered if they would've ended up with an addled ghost, or no ghost at all.

As her hopes of an easy answer faded, Cin looked at her mother.

Charity nodded. "Why don't I stay here with her for a while? She appeared sharp when we got here. That's not the case, but I might be able to get the info out of her with a little time and effort."

"Thanks, Mom." Cin pushed off the table she'd been leaning against. The fact there had been three women who took the jewelry class, although they didn't know which one, made a little sense. Tia Stone might've been one of the women, and the other two might have been other practitioners who worked with Stone as the start of a coven. It would explain some things, but it didn't put them any closer to finding all the answers.

"Vivian, it was nice to meet you." Cin smiled at the older woman.

"Nice to finally meet you too, Charity's daughter. Keep an eye out for my crosses, there're lots of them around town." Her face was still relaxed and her eyes not totally focused.

As Cin left the art room and headed back to the lobby, a woman started screaming and a pair of orderlies ran down the hall as fast as they could. It made her shiver. She hoped she and Chad never had to resort to assisted living facilities as they got older. Somehow, she doubted there were places where a witch and a werewolf would be welcome.

## 22

Cin turned toward the road as the sound of a heavy truck coming toward them drew her attention. A rooster tail fanning out behind the truck spoke of how dry things in the valley were.

"Looks like we've got supplies," RJ said from beside Cin. "About time."

"Yeah." Cin shrugged. "I can't believe after the power company took three days to get the new transformer put in, then the lumber company was out of sheetrock, and took another three days to get it in and out to us." She'd been thinking back on Kama's warning. They had three more days until the full moon. Everything was going to come to a head and she was going to be without Chad, unless they could figure it out before then, and they were at a dead end as far as she could tell. They'd researched the symbols from the charms as best they could, but hadn't found anything useful.

"I'll go tell them where to put everything." RJ headed down the porch steps. "Did Chad get hold of the rest of the crew about working this afternoon?"

"Yeah. He said they should be here by one, and he'd be back from Wolf Creek by noon." She glanced at her watch; it was nearly eleven.

"Sounds good. We'll get this unloaded and have time to get that door in the basement ripped open." RJ made it to the yard and hurried across to the big flatbed turning into the driveway. He waved them down the drive and toward the back of the house. After a bit of a debate, they'd decided it was the best place to stage the building supplies. Although it made sense to Cin and RJ, Chad had wanted everything in the driveway alongside the house. One advantage to having a third voice was she and Chad didn't get stuck in lively discussions about what to do during a build as much.

Instead of standing around watching men work, which had its advantages, Cin headed back into the house and down into the basement. None of them had bothered to come out until the supplies had been delivered, beyond a short visit after the power was back on, so they could finish clearing the master bathroom. Even though they'd been busy, Cin had almost felt like they'd been avoiding the place for the fear that something was going to show its face and they'd have another magical menace to deal with. Luckily, no more transformers had blown and burned down businesses.

As she turned on the basement lights, Cin thought things looked rather bright. When she stopped and thought about it, it was one of the best-lit basements she'd ever been in. A couple of banks of florescent bulbs with no covers blazed so brightly that there weren't any shadows except under the shelves that lined the walls.

She walked over and looked up at the black paint they'd smeared over the trap symbol, effectively erasing that part of the spell. It was still odd that Lucille had stopped over the exact spot where the matching symbol had been on the bedroom floor. Sure there was a chance it had just been luck that made her stop there with her silver-toed western boots, but it was too much luck. At least the spell was destroyed and wouldn't bother anyone ever again.

"Cin, you down here?" RJ called from the open door into the kitchen.

"Yeah, I'm down here." Cin walked away from the defunct spell and over to the locked door. She turned the knob again, and it wouldn't budge. The cool metal of the knob was nearly cold, but they were in the basement. She glanced at her hand. There wasn't any dust on it. Although she knew several of them had tried the door, she couldn't recall there ever being dust on it. In a house, in a part of the country known for dust, surrounded by shelves that had been covered in several inches of it, they hadn't stopped to think that the door that wouldn't open was dust free.

"RJ, do you remember if there was dust or dirt on this knob the first time you tried it?" She stepped back and pointed to the door.

"Ah…" RJ cocked his head and looked thoughtful. "You know I can't say. Might be something to ask Chad."

"I don't remember there being dust on the door, or the knob. That's weird."

"That's weird," he echoed. Then he held up his reciprocating saw. "Then let's get this door out of the way and see what's behind it. The delivery guys will be done in a few minutes. Chad showed up and said he'd handle it."

"Good." Then Cin looked toward the stairs. "You don't think he's going to try and have them put the stuff in the driveway?"

RJ shook his head. "I had the first pallet of stuff unloaded before he got here. I don't think the guys will be happy if he changes his mind about where it's going."

Pursing her lips, Cin nodded and turned back to the door. "Good for you."

Firing up the saw, RJ grinned. "Thanks. Sometimes timing is everything."

Cin didn't say anything as RJ started cutting. It would've been a little faster if they'd brought a chain saw, but the saws-all cut through the door until it thunked against something solid and sparks flew.

"What was that?" Cin stared as RJ pulled the saw back and pulled out his cellphone.

He flicked the flashlight app on and shone it into the cut he'd made. Something glistened behind the wood. RJ frowned. "Metal-core door? Who puts a metal-core door in a basement, and then covers it over with a thick veneer?"

Cin shrugged. "Your guess is as good as mine, but I want to get on the other side of that door even more now."

RJ turned his head and tapped on the doorframe. Then he nodded. "This seems like regular wood. That I can get through without having to go get a different blade." He turned the saw back on, tilted it as a different angle and set to cutting around the kick plate. Within a couple of minutes, he had that part of the frame ready to pop out when they pulled on the door.

"What's going on?" Chad asked as he came down the steps.

"Steel-plated door." Cin pointed to the door. "RJ got creative in getting it open."

"Who would put a—"

Cin cut him off. "We already asked that. We don't know."

"Let's see what they were hiding." RJ grabbed the handle and pulled.

The door swung open and the part of the jamb that had held the kick plate clattered to the floor. A dark tunnel stretched out before them.

"I'll be right back with flashlights." Chad dashed up the stairs.

RJ swung his phone around and activated the flashlight app again. The beam wasn't bright enough to see very far. "I think waiting is probably the better thing to do."

A strange chill flowed out of the tunnel and wrapped itself around Cin. She crossed her arms and shuddered. "Yeah. That's a good idea."

Chad jumped from the top of the stairs and landed on the floor next to them.

On instinct, as her adrenaline spiked, Cin swung hard and caught him in the shoulder.

"What was that for?" He rubbed his shoulder as he handed a flashlight to RJ.

"You scared me, that's what it's for. Why didn't you walk or run down the stairs like a normal person?" Her heart still pounded like crazy.

"But I'm not normal." He handed her a flashlight. "Full moon's only a couple days away. I'm feeling a lot more wolfie than normal this month."

"Okay. I get it, but keep as normal as possible." Cin turned her flashlight on and pointed it down the tunnel.

RJ did the same. "Do you two even know what normal is?"

Chad turned on his light. "Not in a long time. College. I think we did normal in college."

Cin frowned at the two of them. "Normal is boring, but we can do levels of normal, like not scaring the piss out of people who just opened a steel door in a house that's had magical traps and skeletons."

"Okay. Point made." Chad held up his hands in surrender. "Now let's go take a look down here and see what we've uncovered this time."

Although she really didn't want to, Cin followed as Chad went into the darkness. If he stumbled into another magical defense, she needed to be there to help him get out. She wasn't in the mood to lose a husband, even one who got overly furry a couple nights a month.

"Okay, I guess the answer to this is the same person who put a steel-core door in a basement, but who builds a tunnel like this under a house out in the middle of the country in southern Colorado?" RJ asked after they'd gone a couple hundred feet along and still hadn't found the end of the tunnel.

"Drug runners, human traffickers, those are the first two that come to my mind," Chad said.

"People who don't want to deal with a couple feet of snow to go visit the neighbors," Cin threw out, although she didn't really think that was the answer.

"We are heading in the general direction of Sheriff

Jackson's old house," Chad said. "But I think he might've mentioned this when we were digging up the skeletons."

"How do you know that?" Cin asked.

"Werewolves have a very good sense of direction," Chad replied. "We're about at the edge of our property right now."

"And we've got a T in the tunnel." RJ stopped and pointed his light down two tunnels.

"Curiouser and curiouser." Cin frowned. Her nerves were already on edge and more tunnels were not helping. There was no way she was going to do the stupid horror movie thing and split up. They were all staying together.

"We're sticking together," Chad echoed her thoughts. "I say we go left, north."

"I get that you're a werewolf and all, but that's still amazing," RJ said.

Chad shrugged. "Does it help that I was good with directions before the attack?"

Cin laughed. "As long as you had your GPS on. How many times did you get lost on our honeymoon?"

"Hey." Chad pointed at her. "We were both young, and we were in a strange town, and that was before Google maps."

"That's not what you said at the time." Giving Chad a hard time helped her relax. It was closer to their normal life than hiking through an underground tunnel hoping not to run into more magical traps.

"Technology does make the world a lot easier." RJ walked past Chad and kept on going down the tunnel.

They fell silent as they walked along. Although it appeared to be a simply-dug tunnel, there weren't any signs of collapse or disrepair. Even though the dirt didn't hold any residue, Cin wondered if someone had used magic to carve out the tunnel. It was way beyond what she could do, even with the help of her mother and daughters, but she'd heard rumors of powerful covens being able to do major working like the tunnel. They already had a lead that there had been at least three women working together. If Mr. Stone, and any other men involved with the women were also part of the group, they could have access to a lot of power. If they were dealing with people used to that kind of power, they might also be able to shield themselves enough she couldn't detect them.

Power danced across Cin's body.

She froze.

"Guys, stop." Her voice came out as barely a whisper.

RJ and Chad turned back toward her, keeping their flashlights down so they didn't destroy her night vision.

"What's wrong?" Chad asked.

"Power. We've walked into something." She closed her eyes and tried to feel the magic. It was raw, prime energy, like drinking water straight from a spring coming out of a rock.

"What kind of something?" RJ glanced around, flashing his light off the walls. "I'm not seeing anything obvious."

Cin shook her head. "I don't think it's obvious, unless you're sensitive to magical power." The power wasn't coming from the walls; it was like it was running along the tunnel floor, just inches under her feet. With a deep breath, she forced her mind deeper. Power coursed through her. It felt like she was standing in a cold fast-running mountain stream at the same time she grabbed hold of a live wire.

"What in the world." She jerked her perception back to the real world.

Chad touched her arm. "Hon, what's wrong?"

Cin cocked her head. "Not wrong, but I think I know why this property is important, or should I say this tunnel. I mean I guess if someone were strong enough they could pick up on this from the house, or even the road, but this is so strong, so raw."

"Cin." Chad snapped his fingers in her face. "You're

babbling. Focus, hon."

Cin shook her head. "Sorry. Okay. I don't know if RJ's ever heard of them in AJ's research, but I know Chad doesn't know what ley lines are."

"Sources of magical power?" RJ asked. "I've read the theories."

"They're more than theories." Cin knelt and put her hand on the tunnel floor. "We're standing a foot or so over one. And unless I miss my guess, this one is really strong."

"What do you mean, guess?" Chad raised an eyebrow as he looked at her. "Are you sure or not?"

"Not a type of magic I'm used to dealing with." Cin stood and dusted off her hands. "I draw my power from the ambient elemental energy around me. Sometimes I might be able to sense the air line a few blocks from the house, but this is a lot more powerful than that. It's raw water."

"More stable too, I bet." RJ closed his eyes and after a second nodded, like he was trying to sense the line too.

"Yeah. Air lines come and go fairly regularly." Cin wished there was a physical manifestation of the magic where it would be easier to have the guys see what she could sense. "The question that I have going through my head, is this line something worth killing over?"

"How could a witch or coven use this power?" Chad asked. "Is it something dangerous?"

"Yes," Cin and RJ said at the same time.

"Is it something they would kill over?" Chad was quickly switching in major cop-mode, something he was prone to doing on the days leading up to the full moon. Cops and werewolves had a lot in common.

"That's what we've got to figure out." Cin shone her light past RJ, wishing she could see farther down the tunnel. They had to get to the end at some point, and maybe there would be more answers there.

# 23

Cin rapidly grew tired of trudging down the tunnel. The energy that marked the water ley line hadn't last too long, signifying they walked across it, and not down. If she was going to set up something magical, it would be in the line, and not away from it, unless there was something bigger farther down the tunnel.

Chad hummed and looked around.

"What's up?" Cin didn't feel anything out of the ordinary, although she wasn't totally sure what ordinary should be in a tunnel a dozen feet underground.

"I'm fairly sure we just left the property. Still heading north." Chad pulled out his phone and frowned. "It would be nice if these things worked better underground."

"But they don't." RJ panned his flashlight off the tunnel walls and nothing flashed, sparkled, or otherwise stood out in the dirt. "I'd love to know how this tunnel was made. It's too regular to be naturally occurring."

"I bet it was magic, but magic that strong would take a really powerful coven to pull off." Cin didn't want to run into the coven capable of doing that.

RJ frowned and nodded. "Or a major vampire lord or lady."

"Have you run into vampires too?" Chad asked.

"AJ met one up in Denver," RJ explained. "Seemed like a fairly nice fellow. He was asking AJ to stop digging into vampire facts since they were just as happy with vampires being fictional to most people."

"I can see that." Chad glanced around more, getting

increasingly nervous. "It's why the paranormals haven't come out yet. I bet we will at some point. Right now…" he spread his hands to leave a question hanging in the air.

"Maybe if more paranormals were accepted by the general public as real, we wouldn't be traipsing down this tunnel looking for clues about who used magic to kill people." Cin realized she sounded more tired than she really was. She wanted to wrap things up so they could finish the house without any more fears of spells going off or finding more bodies. The tunnel they were walking down would've been a much better place to discard the bodies from the backyard, if it had been there before they were killed.

Waves of heat poured over her and Cin stopped in her tracks and stared around. It was like she'd just walked into the center of an oven set on high.

Chad stopped and looked back at her. "What's up?"

"If the two of you aren't feeling that, I'm going to say we just walked into a fire ley line." Cin hoped they were going across it like they had the water line and she could get out of it quickly. The heat blasting around her made her massively uncomfortable.

"There's a bit of a tingle of something," RJ said. "But you're the major witch around here."

Cin shook her head and kept walking past him. "I don't think I'm very major compared to the people who did this. They had the power to make this tunnel along at least two ley lines."

"Maybe they tapped the lines to make the tunnel." RJ lengthened his stride and caught up to her. "My understanding of magic says that would help."

"Right, if you can tap the lines. That takes training and practice. I never took the time to do more than occasionally pull from an air line, and even then, it was more power than I had use for." Cin didn't want to think about what a coven willing to kill would do with the power of the lines they were crossing. It could be handing a teenage boy a rocket launcher and telling him to shoot whatever he wanted.

Chad drew in a sharp breath, then took a couple of short sniffs. "Wait. I smell blood."

Cin came to a stop, her heart sinking. "Blood?"

With another sniff, Chad nodded. "But it's old blood, not new."

"How old?" RJ asked.

"Hard to tell. The rusty smell is faint." Chad took the lead. "That could be due to age, or distance, but it's not fresh, it has a dryness to it."

"I suppose that should make me feel better." Cin followed after him. She wasn't looking forward to finding another body. Sheriff Jackson was sure to enjoy getting it out of the tunnel and back to the house, unless it would just be easier to call in the backhoe and dig down to it from above.

As they went along, the heaviness of the ground around them weighed in on Cin. She started to sweat again, even though they weren't even close to the fire ley line. They were deep in the earth and that power surged around her, threatening to suffocate her. Her breath came in short gasps and she grabbed hold of RJ.

"What's wrong?" RJ looked at her. "Another ley line?"

"Maybe." Cin gasped out. "Ground's closing in on me. I don't know if I can make it through this one."

Chad came back and took her other hand. "Hang on, Babe. We'll get through this one like we got through the other ones. RJ and I are here for you."

She squeezed both their hands. "Thanks." A quiet steady power rolled off RJ that offset the wild energy that always poured off Chad the closer they got to the full moon.

With each step, the earth power grew stronger. It was so foreign it was suffocating. She desperately wanted out of the tunnel and back into the open air outside. Everywhere there was just dirt and rocks pressing in on her. It was like a giant made of dirt was pressing down on her head, trying to cover her in soil to make her a part of it and never let her go.

She stumbled.

"Do you need me to carry you?" Chad stepped closer and wrapped his arm around her waist.

"No." Cin grasped out as she took a deep breath and steeled her will. "I'll make it. I have to." They didn't know what they were trudging into. She wasn't about to have Chad encumbered with her weight if they might need his hands free.

"We're here." RJ's simple, pure power helped push back the earth, but not much, not enough. He was like a candle in a tornado. It wouldn't take much to overcome him and she desperately needed everything he could give her to bolster her strength.

"Thanks." Cin muttered.

Then as quickly as it hit her, they were clear of the line. She stopped and took a deep breath, feeling more whole and safe than she had seconds before. Turning back around, she tried to see anything in the flashlight beam that would warn her before she stumbled back into it. There was no difference in the tunnel. The ley line existed on another plane and only magically sensitive people like herself would be able to feel it.

"You okay?" Chad asked.

Cin nodded. "Yeah, we're clear of the line. That one was a lot more powerful than the other two were."

"I thought we'd cleared it." RJ glanced around. "I didn't notice it at first, but outside of it, I can tell there was a...pressure...there that isn't here, or on the other side."

"Right." Cin sighed, pushing new fear of being buried alive aside. "Let's get through this so we can get out. I hope there's an exit at the end of this tunnel."

"That would be nice, but it might be a little too much to ask." Chad turned back to the way they were going. "I bet we have to come back through here."

Cin shot the earth line a parting glare, and followed her husband and handyman deeper into the tunnel.

A few feet from the earth line, the tunnel T-ed again.

"Which way?" Chad asked.

Cin panned her light down both tunnels and sighed. "Really? Can't anyone just do things in a straight fashion?"

"Sometimes the path walked is a form of magic in its own way." RJ tapped his flashlight, like he was getting nervous.

"Which way is the blood scent coming from?" Cin asked.

Chad pointed to the right. "That way."

"Then we go that way." Cin wished she felt more confident about what they were doing. Disappearing in the tunnel wasn't how she wanted her story to end. She still had the girls to finish raising, and didn't want to end up like her mother, spending years haunting her children.

The tunnel didn't go long before it turned, thankfully not with a T, but they followed through more turns that were very odd after the tunnel had gone on straight for so long.

"We've entered a labyrinth," RJ said.

"Like the minotaur?" Chad asked.

"Yes." RJ frowned. "Labyrinths and mazes were very popular back in England among people who wanted safe places to do magic where they wouldn't be found out. In some legends by walking a maze in a certain pattern, the practitioners could transcend to another dimension."

Cin wrapped her arms around her as a chill shot through her. "I'm not going to be pleased if we can't get home."

"The European mazes often had gates in them so the path could be changed and only one path would lead to another plane." RJ tapped the wall as they turned another corner. "So far we haven't encountered any gates or doors that could be opened or closed to create another path."

"So this labyrinth just stays in this dimension," Chad said. "That's good, 'cause the dried blood scent is getting stronger."

Wishing they'd thought to bring guns, swords, knives, anything beyond flashlights, Cin didn't say anything. It wasn't identical to the power of the ley lines, but the feeling of power building up around her was growing with every step. She just hoped that when they reached the center of the labyrinth they would end up with answers as opposed to more questions. She was tired of not getting answers.

"Whoa." Chad stopped in front of her as they turned the next corner.

"What?" Cin eased past him and stopped dead in her tracks. She wasn't sure what she was expecting at the center of the maze they found themselves in, but the huge stone altar that looked like something off a Mayan pyramid wasn't it.

"Where did that come from?" RJ muttered from next to Cin.

"That's where the blood smell is coming from." Chad took a cautious step toward the altar.

Cin put out an arm stopping him. "No. We've already hit one trap for non-humans, this is a great place for more." She wished their lights would reach to the far walls, but they barely made it past the altar. Looking along the walls she could see, there were no other passageways coming in. "Chad, stay here. RJ, unless there's something non-human about you that you haven't told us, come with me."

RJ raised his flashlight-free hand. "I'm as human as they come, although I'm not sure that's always a good thing."

Chad laughed. "I'm with you there."

"Okay." Cin rolled her eyes, not always understanding men's need to make jokes at inopportune times. "Chad, you get to guard the door. RJ, let's see what we can find. If we decide it's safe, then Chad can come help us look over the altar."

"Okay." RJ followed Cin as she started around the room.

It was close to a perfect circle. Again, Cin couldn't help but think that someone had used a lot of magic to build the place, but why?

"Cin," Chad called her from where he stood in the entrance to the room. "I think you're right under the river."

Cin waved her flashlight so the beam was across the ceiling. "Going that way?"

"Yeah." Chad nodded.

"The river crosses the altar?" Cin muttered. The Rio Grande was just feet above them. That made her nervous. It wouldn't take much to flood the labyrinth and tunnel they'd come down. The smooth tunnel walls… had a water mage used the power of the river to carve everything out? Had someone found a dried-up underground passage and made use of it? There were still a lot of questions.

RJ glanced up. "But if that's the case, why don't we have dripping and seeping? I would think the river would make everything damp."

"Damp. You're right, and the air down here is more humid than up above." If Cin hadn't been so focused on getting answers, she might've turned and run all the way back to the house and sealed up the basement door to the point it could never be opened again.

"Let's keep going," RJ walked on.

Not wanting him to get too far ahead of her, Cin followed. About a third of the way along the wall, the warm tingle of the fire line spread through her again. It drove the dampness from the air.

"That was the fire line again, wasn't it?" RJ asked.

Cin nodded. "Yes." She glanced across the chamber. "I bet it crosses the river over the altar." Inwardly she groaned. The odds just got larger that they would have to deal with the earth line again, and probably an air line too. The altar was at the ley line convergence, a powerful node of magical energy—power that the killer had been using and that they had wandered into unsuspecting.

"That's not good." RJ continued around the room.

They reached the point they couldn't see the light from Chad's flashlight, when RJ stopped. "We've got another tunnel here."

A tendril of the earth line, smaller than the main part that they'd passed through earlier, ran through the chamber, right before Cin reached the new tunnel. It was only a foot or so wide, easy enough to traverse, but if she'd stood there too long, the feeling of claustrophobia that had hit her earlier would've returned. She walked until she was sure she was beyond it.

Cin wanted to know where the other tunnel led, but didn't want to separate any farther from Chad. They hadn't encountered any other magic than the ley lines, but she wasn't sure that the power of the lines might not be enough to block her from sensing other lesser magics.

"I don't like that." Cin shone her light down the new tunnel.

"I agree." RJ sighed. "But let's just work this chamber for now."

"Sounds like a plan." Cin wanted to get back to Chad, then check out the altar. She supposed it was too much to ask for there to be a coven directory on a shelf under the altar that spelled out everyone who was part of the circle who had crafted the underground complex and left skeletons in the backyard of their current project.

They passed through the other side of the fire line, and were heading toward Chad's light, when RJ grabbed Cin's arm. "Hold on. Someone's coming."

Cin stopped and glanced back toward the tunnel they hadn't gone down. She could just make out the sound of running steps coming toward them. Since she didn't have Chad's enhanced hearing, she couldn't be sure of how many people were rushing their way, but was fairly sure it was just one.

"Chad! Be careful, we're not alone down here." If someone was running their way, they must've tripped some kind of magical alarm that Cin hadn't sensed. She was getting really tired of magic she wasn't familiar with that she kept stumbling through.

"I know." Chad's voice was low and gruffer than normal. He sounded like he was starting a change. So close to the full moon, it could be really dangerous for him to lose his grip on his humanity, it could also be deadly for anyone who stood against them.

Again, Cin wished they had more than just their flashlights.

"Here." RJ pushed a screwdriver into her hand. "It's not much."

"But it's something." Cin almost kissed his cheek. A screwdriver wasn't the same as a dagger, but would still make a point against a foe if they came to hand-to-hand blows. There was a faint tingle to the screwdriver. She instantly wanted to know more, but didn't think it was the right time to ask.

"Exactly." RJ held up his own screwdriver.

Cin's heart pounded heavily as the footsteps grew louder, sounding more and more like just one set, but that didn't do much to stop the butterflies in her stomach. The odds were, the person racing toward them had had a hand in crafting the maze and tunnels and knew the place's secrets. She was about to face off against a powerful practitioner with nothing but a flashlight, a screwdriver, and a handyman to win the fight.

## 24

The running stopped, and a soft glow came from the tunnel they'd passed a few minutes earlier. Cin turned off her flashlight, not wanting to alert the person or persons to her location.

Next to her, RJ did the same. "If the light gets too bright, don't look directly at it."

Cin nodded. "You either."

Seconds later, Lucille Jackson strolled into the chamber, her hand held up with a soft ball of magical light spreading out around it. "Cinnamon Kilkari...how nice of you...to wander down...into my web." The woman stepped calmly, although she was still slightly out of breath from her run down the tunnel.

The fire ley line blazed with power, flooding the entire chamber with light.

"Crap." Cin blinked quickly, hoping the spots before her eyes cleared in time. She didn't want to face Lucille being blind, not that she was sure she had a chance against a woman powerful enough to use a fire ley line as mood lighting.

"That's bright," RJ complained.

Across the room, a howl sounded right before a gun shot rang out.

Cin whirled to the deadly crack.

"That's far enough, Kilkari!" Sheriff Jackson shouted as Cin's vision cleared. "I knew to bring silver bullets."

There hadn't been a sound of pain, or the distinctive thunk of a bullet hitting flesh, but Cin stared across the chamber nonetheless.

Chad stood, his black tail fluffed out and straight behind him as he glared at Sheriff Jackson.

"It's been a long time since we killed a werewolf down here." Lucille strolled across the chamber like she owned the place, and in many ways she did. "Or a witch for that matter." She looked at Cin. "For some reason, the past couple of years the paranormal communities have been avoiding Cottonwood... well, other than those who were born here, or that rogue wolf who tore into your husband. It's made finishing my spells difficult. I needed more power, special power. Thank you for bringing it to me."

Cin turned from Chad and focused on Lucille. "Finish your spells, what are you talking about?"

Lucille laughed. "Nothing I'd expect you to understand. You're still in this dried-up little bump in the road. Some of us have plans for bigger things. But bigger things mean rubbing elbows with bigger people, and for that, I need more power. Power you three are going to provide." She looked at RJ. "Even this little guardian can give more than he realizes."

Guardian? Cin frowned. What was Lucille going on about?

She knew the woman wanted out of Cottonwood, a lot of people did. They didn't see the simple beauty of the place, but most weren't willing to kill to do it.

Lucille stopped walking a few feet from Cin and RJ. "Now, if you would both be so kind as to walk over to the altar, that's where the power of your deaths will give me the most power."

"And if we don't want to?" RJ glared at her.

"There are ways of making you, although a willing sacrifice is so much more powerful." Lucille smiled, like she was looking forward to them struggling and fighting her.

Across the chamber, Chad's growls were loud enough to carry to Cin. She desperately wanted to turn toward and run toward him, but there was no way she was going to take her eyes off Lucille.

In Cin's hand, the screwdriver RJ had given her vibrated more, like something was activating dormant magic.

Lucille's pointed her non-glowing hand at Cin. "Now, move." There was a magical compulsion in the words. It tugged at Cin's mind, but the screwdriver shook more violently in her grasp.

Cin cocked her head and spread her feet a little, taking a firm stance against the woman and her magic. "No."

"I said, move!" Lucille's words washed over Cin like a tidal wave.

They shook her and for a moment, she thought she was going to take a step toward the altar whether she liked it or not.

"She said no!" RJ leaped at Lucille, swinging his flashlight toward her head.

Lucille's glowing hand flared and the power from the earth around them rose up, a gravelly hand shot up out of the cavern floor and grabbed hold of RJ, stopping him in mid-jump. He grunted in pain and hung with the earthy fist holding him tight. His flashlight was still raised like he was going to hit Lucille with it.

"You're in over your head, handyman." Lucille turned her attention back to Cin.

"Maybe not." Cin held up the screwdriver that was still quivering and had taken to glowing. She walked toward Lucille. "You know, climbing the magical ladder was my mother's thing, not mine. I don't pretend to understand why you want to go to Denver, or maybe New York and try to be a big fish in their pond. But, I do understand that we are going to find a way to stop you."

"She's right." RJ threw the flashlight and it caught Lucille in the head.

Cin jumped like RJ had, jabbing down with the

screwdriver. She caught Lucille in the shoulder.

"Lucille!" Jackson shouted from the far side of the chamber.

Chad howled.

Two shots rang out.

The screwdriver sank to the handle and power from the ley lines acted like it was a lightning rod for their power. As if they had wills of their own, they lashed out at Lucille.

The witch screamed as the power flooded into her body. She glowed with otherworldly power and exploded.

Turning, Cin tried to shield her eyes from the brightest light she'd ever seen. Then darkness engulfed the chamber. She waited a minute before clicking on her flashlight. Panning it in front of her where Lucille had been moments before, she couldn't see any sign of the woman. The screwdriver lay where she'd stood. It had stopped glowing and vibrating.

"We might need more tools." RJ beat against the earthen hand still holding him a couple of feet off the ground.

Chad's howl of a successful hunt filled the chamber.

Cin spun in his direction and in the beam of her light, a huge black wolf stood over the prone body of Sheriff Jackson.

"Chad! No!" Cin ran across the chamber. She couldn't imagine how Chad was going to feel if he'd either killed the sheriff, or worse, turned him into a werewolf. But he'd been threatening Chad while his wife came at Cin and RJ.

With eyes that looked nothing like her husband's regular blue gaze, the wolf glared at her.

Skidding to a stop a few feet away, Cin stretched out a hand to the wolf. "Come on, Chad. I know you're in there. It's not the full moon yet. Fight this. RJ and I are safe."

Chad's growl grew again. He looked at Cin and then down at Jackson. Again he raised his muzzle and howled. It was a lonely heartbreaking sound.

## Second-Story Hex

Cin's fingers brushed Chad's ear. He snapped at her, then froze.

It was all she could do to not withdraw her hand. She knew how dangerous he could be, but she needed to reach her husband under the fur. "Chad. It's okay. We're safe. Come back to me."

Taking a couple of steps back, away from her, Chad whined. Then he spun and took off down the tunnel they'd come in. His lonely howl reverberated along the tunnels and quickly faded away.

Ignoring the urge to scream, Cin knelt next to Sheriff Jackson. His throat had been torn out. At least Chad hadn't infected the man with his form of lycanthropy. She'd spent many hours over the years since the attack talking with Chad about his change and how he never wanted to infect another person with lycanthropy. In his own way, he'd saved Jackson from a fate worse than death.

"He's dead." Cin stood and walked back toward RJ. "Got any ideas?"

"There's a sledgehammer in my truck, if Chad can find his way back to human, he can get me out of here." RJ spread his hands. "Other than that, I think you're going to need to call the authorities and get this mess sorted out. We might also want to find a way to collapse these tunnels."

"Yeah, that's a mess too, isn't it?" Cin stooped and picked up the screwdriver. "What's with this thing?"

"It's thrice blessed." RJ awkwardly shrugged. "I kinda did it on impulse. Took it to a priest, a shaman and a wizard. Between the three of them, they promised there would be very little evil that could stand against it. I might want to get a few more of them."

Cin nodded. "Yeah. 'Cause I might just have to keep this one. Not that I anticipate dealing with more power-hungry witches in the future."

"I hope not." RJ tried to shift and frowned. "Maybe you

can go get my hammer and your husband to get me out of here. I've got itches building up that I really need to scratch."

Picking up the flashlight RJ had thrown at Lucille, Cin turned it back on and handed it to him so he wouldn't be in the dark when she left.

"I'll see what I can do." Cin was thankful they hadn't just been randomly turning down the tunnels as she headed back toward the house. It would be easy enough to find her way out. What she wasn't sure was how hard it was going to be to find Chad. In his wolf form, he was a lot faster than any human and he was stressed from killing Jackson. He could run for hours.

## 25

Cin couldn't remember when the dry dusty air of Cottonwood tasted as good as it did as she walked out of the Stone house. She stepped out onto the porch and took a deep breath. Twilight spread fire across the western horizon. There were few sights as impressive as the sunsets in the San Luis Valley.

As she turned from the light show, Cin realized that a collection of black Suburbans clogged the driveway behind their car and RJ's blue truck.

"Cin!" Chad ran toward her, once again in one of RJ's plaid flannel work shirts.

Several people in dark suits stepped aside as he went past them, then hurried after him.

"Chad, you're okay." She hugged him as he swept her up in his arms and kissed her. "I was afraid I was going to have to wait for you to come home."

"Yeah." Chad set her down. "If it hadn't been for these guys, you would've."

"Ma'am." A tall, broad-shouldered man appeared behind Chad. "We'd like to talk to you."

"We need to get RJ's sledge hammer down to him so we can bust himself out." Cin turned toward the man and a chill went through her. She knew instantly he was a werewolf, a very powerful and dangerous werewolf. Since when did werewolves show up looking like FBI or secret service?

"RJ? Oh, Regulous Jetter Samson, the owner of the blue Dodge Ram." The big werewolf motioned for two other people in black suits. "Please go into the labyrinth and retrieve Mr. Samson. Take Agent Mays with you. There's still some latent magic waiting around down there."

Cin cocked her head. "What are you people?"

"There's a special task force with the FBI," Chad said. "I'd heard rumors of them."

"And you didn't share this with me?" Cin stomped her foot and fixed him with a hard stare.

Chad shrugged. "Cop talk. And until I got up here and Agent Briar was able to bring me back, I didn't know they were real."

Agent Briar nodded slowly. "And the fewer people who know about us, the better we like it."

"You're not going to try any memory wiping spells or anything like that." Cin put her hand in her jeans pocket. She still had RJ's thrice-blessed screwdriver, would it protect her from such a spell, like it had saved her from Lucille?

"No." Agent Briar put his hands in his pockets and shook his head. "You're members of the paranormal community. We do ask that you don't go spreading word of our existence around, but we only use spells like that on humans whom we deem might be a threat to the community."

"Oh." Cin relaxed a little, but was still relieved by the screwdriver in her pants.

"We do need to thank you for dealing with the threat Lucille Jackson presented to the community. Normally, by the time a witch reaches her power, we have them on our rolls. We've been researching the disappearances in this area for some time."

"The Stones?" Cin glanced at Chad.

"More than that," Chad filled in. "My search of the local database for missing people triggered an alarm at the bureau. Turns out, there's a lot more people missing than what I could find. Mostly migrants and such, people who fly under the normal radar."

## Second-Story Hex

Cin nodded. "Sounded like Lucille had been doing a lot of sacrifices in her little maze down there. She just needed a couple of victims with power." She sighed. "You and me. Although she called RJ a guardian. I'm not totally sure what that means."

Agent Briar cocked an eyebrow. "Mr. Samson is a guardian. That explains a lot."

"Like what?" Cin took a step toward the werewolf, then realized what she was doing and whom she was about to threaten for info, and backed off. She didn't think she really wanted to engage a shadowy agent from the FBI.

"Let's just say we've been a little concerned about Mr. Samson and his writer husband. If he's a guardian, we can relax. I'll have that added to his file." Agent Briar turned and pointed toward their cars. "Why don't you two go rest and we'll have things here wrapped up fairly soon. Your husband says we'll need to handle Sheriff Jackson's body, and disappearance. Don't worry. We've got it covered."

Cin wanted to ask Chad how much he and the FBI wolf had discussed before she made it out of the tunnels, but decided that could wait until they got home. At least the FBI was going to handle all the nitpicky details of the Jacksons and Cin and Chad weren't going to have to worry about what the locals would do. The Cottonwood paranormal community was safe.

She glanced up in the sky; the sun was gone and the Milky Way was slowly coming out. A shooting star raced across the sky. Cin smiled. At least they had just dealt with a simple power-hungry witch and not an alien come to start their conquest of the planet in the valley.

# 26

With her arms full of a tote of cleaning supplies, Cin waited for RJ to unlock the door and open it up. Normally, she would just send in her cleaning crew to do the final once-over before listing a house, but with everything they'd been through since first viewing the place, she wanted to take a personal hand in it. She and the girls had spent the previous night working on special cleaning supplies to make sure everything the least bit magical was gone from the place.

"Doesn't even feel like the same place." RJ turned to take the tote.

Cin shook her head. "I can get it. You know it's amazing how removing tons of sand and black magic can improve the atmosphere of a house."

RJ chuckled. "You have that right. At least the neighbors bought the gas pocket explosion explanation when that FBI witch collapsed the maze and tunnels."

"You'll be amazed what the people around here will believe. You've seen the UFO watchtowers haven't you?" She pointed toward the north east, even though one wasn't within view of the house.

"Yeah. Chad said something about one of those being near an apartment complex you guys just took on."

As she opened the tote, Cin sighed. "That's right. Another of Marzie's finds. The owners are getting older and were looking for a property management firm to take it over. Meana more work for all of us, but at least we don't foot things like repair bills."

## Second-Story Hex

"I think we did a good job on this place, even if I do say so myself." RJ offered to take a couple of bottles from Cin.

Again, she shook her head. Although she didn't doubt that RJ might be able to add a bit of his own guardian magic to her efforts to clean, she wanted to do it herself. She needed to personally make sure that no trace of Lucille and the Stones remained. There were still unanswered questions. The new sheriff, Randy Reynolds, had resorted to dental records to identify the Stones as the skeletons from the backyard, and the bones from the cow pasture had belonged to the last person to rent the second story efficiency from the Stones.

Cin still couldn't figure out how the end table in the efficiency had defied the San Louis dust, and promised to check from time to time, when the place was empty, to see if the phenomenon continued. She wrote off the lights Shelby said people saw as a physical manifestation of the ley line convergence. That might have been how Lucille first found out about it and convinced Jackson to buy the closest house to it. She would still love to know how Lucille, even with the help of a coven, had managed to craft the tunnels and labyrinth, particularly without anyone knowing what was happening.

"RJ, if you'll just follow me around. I'll handle the final cleansing. This lavender, dragon's blood, and lemon mixture should be enough to knock out anything we missed earlier."

Nodding, RJ chuckled. "With the amount of cleansing we've already done on this place, I'd be surprised if any kind of spirit or magic would dare show its face."

"You've noticed Mom's keeping her distance lately, haven't you?" Cin grinned at the memory of Chad's happiness at her mother's announcement that she wouldn't be visiting due to everything Cin had done to purify the place. As a spirit she was much more sensitive to the least little bit of shielding and purifying magic. The fastest way to get her to leave the house for a while was to burn a smudge stick. There had never been a sign of the spirits she'd claimed were living there either. Maybe they'd inadvertently done something that had helped them find rest.

"Yeah, I had. Too bad, she was great at helping me get things lined up just right when there wasn't anyone else around."

"Thanks for letting her do that." Cin started spraying the mixture around the front room. "She really appreciated something new to do."

RJ shrugged. "No big deal. She acts like she's a bit lonely in the afterlife."

"I think she is from time to time." Cin paid special attention to the corners, making sure nothing, not even a few foul words and emotions from construction mishaps, remained.

She moved so slowly that it was nearly dinnertime before she was satisfied with her and RJ's work. The hardwood floors glistened and the wainscoting in the dining area was a perfect accent to the dark windowsills. In the kitchen, the granite counters gleamed as did the stainless-steel appliances and the central lamp that RJ had found in a second-hand shop and refinished.

"I think it'll look better with furniture in it," RJ said as he opened the door for Cin to carry her tote out.

"It will, but right now that's not our worry. In a few years, when we decide it's time to sell it off instead of renting it, then we'll bring in a company to showcase it and make it more appealing to buyers. Until then, we'll do what we can to make sure we get good renters who'll take care of her." Cin finished her last bottle of cleanser on the door, then paused, pulled out a small piece of paper she and the girls had written out the previous evening. It was a simple spell to make sure they'd only get the best renters possible. It would convince people who might misuse the place they didn't want to live there. She didn't do that sort of thing to all the properties they managed, but it was something she did to places they owned.

After the spell was cast, she dropped the paper down between the new recycled porch slats. The paper was one that didn't last long in the elements. It would go back to the planet, leaving no trace it was there, but as it faded, it would keep the spell going, hopefully long enough for them to find renters who would love the place.

Cin smiled at RJ. "Come on, we're supposed to meet AJ, Chad and the girls for steaks to celebrate. I'm looking forward to finally meeting AJ."

RJ nodded. "He's looking forward to meeting you too. He just finished his latest book last night, so we'll be celebrating that too."

"Great." Cin carried the tote down the steps, thankful they didn't have to worry about where to step any longer. The house had been a bit of a struggle, but it was ready for Chad to list it the next day. If they were lucky, it would be a while before they encountered another house that required so much reno, on many levels. But she felt good as they walked back to their vehicles. They'd done an awesome job.

Since it would be dark soon anyway, after she stashed the tote, she glances at RJ. "Do me a favor and grab a hammer. We might as well save a trip out tomorrow and put out the sign."

"Sure." RJ went to his truck as she pulled out the sign. If they were anywhere in the country that had soft soil, they wouldn't need the hammer, but the valley had notoriously hard dirt.

Minutes later the sign was out. The Stone house was finished and up for rent.

Cim's adventures continue in "Watchtower WooWoo".

To keep up with A.M. Burns, visit www.amburns.com and

sign up for his email list.

Each sign up will get a bonus RJ short story

"The Power of Tool"

If you enjoyed "Second-Story Hex" be sure to leave a

review.

A.M. Burns Bio:

A.M. Burns lives in the Colorado Rockies with his partner, several dogs, cats, horses, and birds. When he's not writing, he's often fixing fences, splitting wood, hiking in the mountains, or flying his hawks. He's enjoyed writing since he was in high school, but it wasn't until the past few years that's he's begun truly honing his craft. He is a previous president of the Colorado Springs Fiction Writers Group. www.csfwg.org. Having lived both in Colorado and Texas, rugged frontier types and independent attitudes often show up in his work. You can find out more about A.M. and his writing at www.amburns.com .

Social media links.
Website: www.amburns.com
Email : andy@amburns.com
Facebook: www.facebook.com/authoramburns
Goodreads author page:
http://www.goodreads.com/author/show/5134598.A_M_Bur
ns
Amazon Author Page: http://www.amazon.com/-
/e/B0054EVI6W
Mystichawker Press Author Page:
http://www.mystichawker.com/amburns.html
Colorado Springs Fiction Writers Group
http://www.csfwg.org

Other Books by A.M. Burns

Blood runs deep in Jemez Springs.

Psychic cougar shifter Connor McGriffin is used to his visions leading him around. For years, he's followed them back and forth across the country to the people who need his help. When his comfortable vacation in the mountains is interrupted by a vision of a woman dying, he can't see enough details to find the killer and stop him from striking again. Facing the most dangerous foe he's ever dealt with, Connor needs all the help he can get.

Small town deputy and wolf shifter, Danny Lupan is getting bored of chasing speeders and the occasional drug dealer. When the call comes that Sandoval County has its first murder in years, and it happened in his jurisdiction, he jumps at the chance to find the killer, no matter the danger involved. Little does he know, he might lose his heart, his life, or maybe both.

When a cougar and a wolf join forces, the bad guys better watch out, because the fur's going to fly, in more ways than one.

Join Connor and Danny on their first adventure together in the start of the fast-paced, suspenseful thriller series Shifter Force.

Available in print and Kindle Unlimited.

A war is about to break out, and the combatants are who everyone expects. Can a dragon and a young mage stand in the middle of it and hope to get out alive?

Tal O'Duirwood, druid dragon, enjoys his quiet life of solitude in the Colorado mountains. When the need arises, Tal is the one the Coalition of Magical Creatures calls on to handle problems no one else can. For years he's worked on his reputation as the thing of nightmares for those who step out of the shadows. He never realized what was missing from his life until his gets an assignment to travel to Yellow Sky, Texas and help a witch and her students there stop a vampire invasion. Once there, he finds things were not as he was told. The witch is actually a werecoyote, and one of her students has eyes for Tal. Can Tal help stop the vampires in time to save his blossoming love? Will his heart, so long closed off from the world, be able to open to the touch of the handsome young mage

Available in print and E-book.

# A.M. Burns

For several months, Detective Greg Williams and his partner have been trying to catch the Black Fin gang. Their latest intelligence is good, so they go on their most risky raid yet. But things go horribly wrong. While recuperating from the wounds he received during the botched raid, Detective Williams and his captain realize there might be a leak in the Portland police department. When they begin digging, things get worse for Williams.

At the urging of his captain, Detective Williams heads into the mountains, hoping a little distance from the department will give the Black Fins and their police informants the opportunity to slip up. His working vacation soon takes turns he could never have imagined when he meets the reclusive writer, Ken Draiag, next door, who turns out to be more than Greg ever imagined. But the Black Fins aren't about to let Detective Williams rest, they soon track him down, but with Ken's help, Greg manages to stay alive and fight back as forces he never knew existed reveal themselves to be working against him. Will Greg survive the Black Fins' ultimate plot?

Available in Print and E-book